Larceny in Lubrín

Almería Mysteries Book 1

Nika Grahame

Ilamera Ltd

Paperback ISBN 978-1-915655-01-1

eBook ISBN 978-1-915655-00-4

Contents

1

Start at the End

"I don't get why you have to leave again!" exclaimed twelve-year-old Kelly, pouting as her aunt, Judy Fargo, packed up her beat-up old suitcase yet again.

"I will be back before you know it, Kels, I promise," vowed her aunt. Her frank, honey-coloured eyes were full of love and warmth. "Here, I got you something. So you will always remember that you are in my heart of hearts," she continued, taking something out of her jacket pocket.

"What is it?" asked Kelly, impatiently brushing away her tears, curious in spite of herself.

"It is a half-heart necklace. See," explained Judy, beaming as she gazed into her niece's eyes that mirrored her own, "you wear your half of the pendant and I will wear mine. To remind us of our bond even when we are far apart." Judy lovingly helped Kelly put on the necklace before continuing.

"I will be doing lots of travelling back and forth, Kels. I can't help it. I need to know that you and Lenny will be alright. Mrs Atwood will stay with you guys while I am away. Now, come and give your old Aunt Judy one of your world-famous bear hugs, will you?"

Kelly Simpson, now a grown woman of thirty-six, fingered the old half-heart pendant, tenderly. She basked in the glow of that distant memory she had stored away in the recesses of her mind, along with all the others that were filled with Judy's warmth and love. Kelly hugged herself in an attempt to hold on to that fragment of warmth the memory brought to her heart.

She was grateful for the soft, steady rain that hid her tears as she watched Judy's casket sink deeper and deeper into its final resting place. The grave site itself was situated at the edge of a quaint old church that Aunt Judy would sometimes visit on her way to the beautiful countryside of Lubrín on her trusty bicycle.

Carelessly clawing at the wispy blonde tendrils that clung to the soft contours of her face, Kelly Simpson tried to make sense of the cloud of unanswered questions swarming around in her grief-befuddled mind. She felt somewhat far-removed from her surroundings – like she was swimming in a murky, unfamiliar lake. This was mainly because she was in the midst of a cacophony of unintelligible whispers of condolences from well-meaning strangers with whom she hadn't the slightest connection. Forlorn and lost, she wondered, not for the first time, what Judy Fargo's life had been like when she wasn't being Kelly's whole world.

"This must all seem a bit surreal to you right now, I expect," came the melodious voice of the lanky, exotic-looking woman standing beside her. Her accent was strange, with a cosmopolitan flavour – it was distinctly English; London to be precise. But Kelly detected a strong provincial Spanish influence that gave the speaker an allure that went well with her sophisticated, statuesque appearance.

"You speak English," exhaled Kelly in relief, not realising that she had been holding her breath in awkward silence the whole time.

"I'm Camilla López, friend and employee of your late aunt. I am sorry to meet under such dire circumstances. But I want you to know that you can count on me to assist with anything and everything you need." Her luminous, dark eyes shone with fierce loyalty to Judy as she spoke, and that cherry red lip colour she wore with such grace seemed to be the only colour for miles around. It somehow offered a respite from the shroud of mourning that enveloped them.

"I am sorry that I didn't make it back to meet you at the airport. You must have felt so lost. I had to run a special errand that took a bit longer than expected," she explained vaguely. However, her disarming smile instantly set Kelly at ease.

"You worked with my aunt? You must be Aunt Judy's 'Camy' then. How do you do? I remember hearing my aunt talking with you when she would come visit us back home. I am pleased to meet you, Camilla."

Kelly took in the chic silhouette of the self-assured and poised Miss Camilla López and couldn't help feeling somewhat frumpy and drab in comparison. Despite her slight build and five-foot-three height, Kelly preferred to wear loose-fitting clothing made from soft, natural fabrics. Her signature hairstyle was a makeshift messy bun held together by a pencil or chopstick, and her cat-eye spectacles left no doubt that she was much more comfortable with cerebral pursuits like puzzles and cryptic brainteasers than being in social settings.

Camilla, on the other hand, seemed to be a social butterfly who thrived on attention. It was hard to believe that she was almost a decade older than Kelly. From what she remembered about the woman, her aunt would entrust the Lubrín office to Camilla whenever she was away.

The overwhelming sense of loss threatened to overtake Kelly, and she was grateful to Camilla for extending her sinewy, well-manicured hand in friendship. She could not quite put her finger on it, but there seemed to lie a festering hostility just beneath the surface of politeness among the other mourners. Maybe I am just being paranoid, Kelly chided herself dismissively.

Camilla made her feel like she was finally part of what was happening around her, whereas just moments ago, she had felt like an outsider looking in. Kelly, dwarfed by Camilla's towering presence, felt like a schoolgirl who had grazed her knee on the field and was being tended to by a knowing coach or school nurse. But the pain ran much deeper than a scraped knee, or any physical injury for that matter. Judy had been a rock and the only family she and Lenny, her older brother, had. She had taken them in when their mum had passed away from a rare form of leukaemia and had raised them as best as she could despite being merely twenty-five years old herself.

"I am sure that this is not how you imagined ushering in the New Year, Kelly," consoled Camilla, draping an elegant arm around Kelly's drooping shoulders. Kelly recalled how she had meticulously planned her New Year's Eve celebration. Her on-and-off boyfriend, Will Holden, had missed a big promotion at work, and she had wanted to cheer him up. So, she had booked a romantic little trip to Achill Island off the Mayo coast of Ireland where they would watch the last sunset in Europe as it is one of the most westerly points in Ireland. She had planned to start the evening at the observation deck overlooking Keel and Achill Head, to take in the sun setting on the old year. Thereafter, they would go pub hopping and end up ushering in the New Year to the sound of a pipe band. And, on New Year's Day, she planned to take him on a romantic stroll along Dugort Beach. She had toyed with the idea of finishing off the morning adventure by taking an icy dip into the Atlantic Ocean on a dare.

Instead, she had spent New Year's Eve booking a plane ticket to Spain to bury the closest thing to a mother she had had since she was ten years old. Will had been surprisingly understanding and had even driven her to the airport. He had been almost consoling – Will was a lot of things, but he was not really the comforting type and did not handle emotional situations well.

Kelly did not realise that she had been crying until Camilla brushed away her tears and gave her a long and much-needed hug. "There, there, now," she said softly, patting Kelly's back comfortingly.

"Why don't you come back to my place tonight?" suggested Camilla, grasping Kelly's elbows firmly. "We can open up a bottle of Judy's favourite wine and celebrate her memory together over some dinner. What do you say?" she cajoled.

"Yes, thank you. I would like that very much, Camilla," sniffed Kelly, grateful for the offer.

"But I don't want to inconvenience you if you've already made dinner plans," she added, as she noticed a fetching younger gentleman waiting discreetly off to the side. He was clearly waiting for Camilla.

"Oh, don't mind him, Kelly. A woman my age needs a distraction or two to keep the blood pumping in her veins. Plus, it helps chase away the chill to have someone to keep me warm in the evenings, you know?" Camilla said with a wink, giving Kelly's arm a gentle squeeze. "Let me quickly get rid of him, and we can get out of here. Give me a moment," she said with an amiable smile that lit up her entire face.

Kelly wondered fleetingly what it must feel like to be able to walk into a room and command the attention of every man present just by existing. It was clear that Camilla was not familiar with rejection of any sort. She watched as Camilla coolly sauntered over to the attractive man dressed in a black tailored suit. His stubbly whiskers failed to hide the strong, chiselled jawline that women found irresistible. Camilla touched him lightly on the arm and whispered discreetly into his ear. He gave her a nod and a peck on the cheek before reluctantly walking away.

Guilt coursed through Kelly's mind, and she was going through a short list of excuses to cancel when Camilla's voice cut into her thoughts. "Ronaldo and I have a casual understanding. It is no problem. Besides, it is better to keep them wanting more, no?"

In her usual take-charge manner, Camilla commandeered Kelly's intense mourning and ensured that she would not sit in the dark alone. It was the least she could do for the woman who had been such a dear and generous friend to her for the past two decades.

"What do you say we get out of here?"

Camilla took Kelly back to the hotel to pack an overnight bag, and they made their way to the residential part of the little town. Even though it was after six-thirty in the evening, the sun still peeked through the rapidly dispersing clouds. Kelly was happy to sit back and take in the scenery while Camilla drove her fire-engine red Peugeot through the narrow, winding streets as the sun set on Kelly Simpson's first day in Lubrín.

"Don't be fooled by the rustic setting. This little town is remarkably quaint and attracts its fair share of visitors during the year. This is precisely why we at Fargo Estate Agents have managed to survive the worst of times in Europe. People want charm they can afford, and we are happy to provide them with a little slice of the continental experience for a fraction of the price. Everyone is happy, and we manage to smile all the way to the bank." Camilla had an easygoing manner of talking about even the most serious and intricate of topics. Kelly could tell that about her already.

Kelly also suspected that while Camilla may be a bombshell with questionable social habits, she sure knew her way around the estate agency business. And Kelly was already depending on Camilla's business smarts to get them through the delicate process of winding down existing deals that were in various stages of completion. Kelly was not exactly familiar with how property sales and acquisitions worked in Spain, and she felt like she would have been taking shots in the dark and hoping for the best if Camilla had not been around to save the day.

Lenny and his wife, Laura, were off on some cycling tour in Africa and Kelly had not even managed to break the news to him, as they would be completely off the grid for the entire week. It was that time of the year when people either got together or scattered to the winds, only to resurface the day before the world went back to business as usual. Kelly kept wondering what really happened to Aunt Judy that fateful afternoon of December 29. She was hoping that Camilla would help her piece the story together.

They finally pulled up to a quaint and beautifully renovated two-storey villa on the edge of Lubrín, alongside the Sierra Filabres mountains. It was not the kind of place in which Kelly imagined Camilla would live. It was remarkably artsy with great attention to detail. This home was designed for convenience and luxury with all the trappings of modern comforts while simultaneously retaining a quaint rustic elegance with typical Spanish design elements. From the tiny silver diamond patterns on the porch and balcony flooring to the massive wrought iron harp-shaped burglar bars on the windows, this villa was steeped in charming Spanish flavour. The Spanish arches inside completed the look.

"Welcome to my humble abode. Mi casa es su casa, my darling," tittered Camilla in her casual, off-handed way. "I met Judy while I was looking to buy a place – and this is what she found for me," she stated grandly, gesturing to the villa. Her eyes shimmered at the memory. "Of course, I gave the place a complete overhaul and made it my very own piece of heaven," she added proudly.

"It is truly exquisite," marvelled Kelly. "Thank you for letting me spend the night here."

"You are most welcome, Kelly darling. Now I will let you get settled in the guest room. You can shower and get into your PJs while I rustle us up some dinner. What do you say?" Then shooed Kelly into the guest room when the younger woman offered to help prepare dinner.

"Nonsense, Kelly. Let me give you a taste of Lubrín hospitality," she insisted.

Kelly showered off the jet lag and the chill from standing in the rain all afternoon. Feeling much warmer and refreshed, she made her way back downstairs and was greeted by the most delicious aromatic smells that made her realise that she hadn't eaten all day. Her stomach gave an appreciative growl, and she helped Camilla set the table while the roasted veggies were still in the oven. Camilla had made an amazing salad to go with it and was just toasting some sort of traditional stuffed bread on the griddle.

"What kind of bread is that? I have never seen it before. What's in it?"

"This is one of my go-to dinner favourites," confessed Camilla with a smile. "It's called hornazo, and it's got everything a gal needs: pork loin, hard-boiled eggs, and – my favourite – chorizo," she added.

"Wow. Sounds like this is a hearty meal by itself, Camilla. This and the salad would have sufficed, you know," chided Kelly.

"I like having something with veggies at dinner. Even if it is a simple veggie soup. There is an interesting story about the origins of the hornazo bread. It isn't from these parts exactly. It is a bread that is traditionally eaten in the Salamanca region at the 'Monday of the Waters' or Lunes de Aguas festival."

"Sounds intriguing," encouraged Kelly, helping herself to some of everything on offer.

"Legend has it that the name of the festival comes from a twisted version of the word enagua, which means petticoat," explained Camilla. "Now, in the olden days, the prostitutes would wear them underneath their dresses. During Lent, all the prostitutes in Salamanca would be sent to the other side of the Tormes River. This was to preserve the spiritual focus of the men in the town during that sacred period of time. Then, on Easter Monday, all the male students of the town would throw a wild party on the banks of the river to celebrate the return of their much-appreciated women of the night, and they would eat hornazo as part of the celebrations."

"Well, I guess they would need all their stamina to give the women a proper welcome late into the night, I expect," added Kelly mischievously, to which they both burst into giggles.

"Come to think of it, a lot of the breads that are prepared around Easter are made with hard-boiled eggs," mused Camilla.

"Actually, I read that in ancient times, all forms of meat-eating were forbidden during Lent." Kelly was glad to have something to add to the discussion. "And that included the consumption of eggs. But that did not stop the hens from laying eggs throughout the month. So the locals would boil them to preserve them, and they would later be used in traditional dishes after the fasting period. Some say that it is probably the reason we celebrate Easter with Easter eggs."

"Wow! That makes a lot of sense. I always wondered about that. I can tell that you are one of those bookworms who just knows a lot about a lot of things; am I right?"

"I guess you could say that," answered Kelly, a deep blush creeping up her face.

"No, don't get me wrong, Kelly. I think that is just one of the obviously fascinating things about you. I remember Judy speaking very proudly of your ability to solve puzzles and learn about all kinds of mysterious things. She was super proud of you both," admitted Camilla, pouring them another glass of the most divine-tasting wine Kelly had sipped in a long time.

"To Judy Fargo, the best aunt and friend in the world," toasted Kelly.

"Salud," replied Camilla, and they clinked glasses.

"And may Judy's legacy continue with your new chapter here," added Camilla.

2

Deluge

"Hello there. This is Will Holden. I am sorry that I missed your call. But if you leave your name and number, I will get back to you as soon as possible."

Kelly had been trying to get a hold of Will all week. He had been quite put out by her decision to remain in Spain indefinitely and, in typical Will Holden style, was ignoring her – making her stew. He often resorted to punishing her for not placing him at the centre of her world. Kelly sometimes wondered what she saw in him at all. Theirs had grown into a relationship of convenience, and she was tired of being the one to make all the effort. But he was the only man who managed to make her feel desirable just as she was. He accepted that she preferred soft, comfortable fabrics and loose-fitting clothing, never trying to get her to wear sexy clothes and spiked heels like some of her exes. And he fed her thirst for puzzles and lateral thinking problems.

Will also respected Kelly's need for discretion, as she had always been rather shy about going public with her relationships, preferring to keep her private life private. They were both fiercely independent and not in the least bit clingy. In fact, Will was something of a cold fish, really. And even though Kelly hated to admit it, she often found herself begging for his attention and affection. As a result, she usually ended up making all the elaborate romantic plans – and at her own cost, of course. And he would deign to avail himself as and when his schedule permitted. Their relationship was always about him and his needs. But Kelly refused to accept any of these truths, despite Lenny and Laura having pointed them out to her repeatedly.

Luckily, her aunt's estate agent business was keeping her thoroughly occupied. Kelly had thrown herself into trying to make sense of the land acquisition and sales laws and taxation system in Spain.

"Maria, please can you check if the certificado urbanìstico is in keeping with the client's intended use for the land for contract 21/02478?" requested Kelly, as politely as she could muster, even though Maria Gonzales was filing her talons for nails and blowing bubbles loudly with the massive wad of gum in her mouth – pointedly ignoring Kelly's request.

"Camilla, could you please help me communicate with Maria? It seems like she doesn't understand what I am trying to ask of her," begged Kelly.

Camilla and Maria then exchanged words in Spanish in what sounded like a heated discussion that ended with Maria glaring at Kelly before stomping out of the office in a dramatic huff.

"*Um*. How about I take over managing the agents from now on, and you deal with the contracts and paperwork, *hmm*?" asked Camilla, an apologetic smile appearing.

So, Kelly studied the paperwork with the help of the translator app on her desktop and left managing Maria to Camilla. It was like wading through a deluge of paperwork anyway, and there were days in which Kelly was ready to throw in the towel.

At last, Will called. It was in the middle of her workday, and she was completely frazzled by a client who had hurled a barrage of what sounded like abuse at her before hanging up abruptly. When the phone rang a second later, Kelly answered apprehensively.

"Hola, hello. Judy Fargo Estate Agents, how may I help you?"

"K-e-l-l! How's my favourite girl holding up?" crooned Will Holden in what he obviously thought was his most alluring voice.

"Hi," answered Kelly, her frustration instantly giving way to a shy, girlish thrill. Camilla, who had been drawing up some documents, looked up from her screen. Recognising that tone all too well, she decided to go out onto the terrace for a smoke and perhaps check in on how Ronaldo was doing.

"I am sorry but I think we've been missing each other over the phone. I tried to return your calls, but it kept going to voicemail. How are you doing out there, Kell?"

"I'm trying to find my feet. There is a lot more paperwork here. Lots of red tape with the law and due process. Do you miss me at all?" she asked coyly.

"Of course I miss you, Kell. When do you think you'll come back?" he asked, a sudden tension in his voice, and he seemed to be holding his breath in anticipation.

"I... I don't think it will be any time soon, I'm afraid, Will. Is there any chance you could swing a visit sometime?" asked Kelly, hopefully.

"Kelly..." He faltered. There was silence as he fumbled for the right words.

"What is it, Will?" Her guard was suddenly up – he never called her Kelly unless something serious was to follow.

"I think it is time I told you the truth. I'm married," he said, simply.

"You're... married?"

The heavy silence threatened to drag on until Will continued. "I've been meaning to come clean about it for a long time now. But I just couldn't seem to find the right moment. Until your move to Spain. It sort of helped me put things into perspective. I don't think I am cut out for a long-distance relationship, Kell."

"Don't you mean a long-distance affair?" bellowed Kelly, suddenly enraged. "How dare you treat me like this, Will? After all this time? You've had almost two years to tell me the truth!"

"I am sorry, Kelly. I just couldn't bring myself to tell you before. But now..." His voice trailed off.

"You mean, now that your mistress has left the country, it is proving more of an inconvenience to keep up the charade? Isn't that what you mean, Will? You are some piece of work, Mr Holden! Please don't ever make contact with me again! Have a wonderful life with your poor, unsuspecting wife!" And with that, Kelly hung up.

Her chest heaved with the thought of how foolish she had been not to have seen the signs. And then, inevitably, the rage turned to heartache – and heartache turned to guilt. She was sobbing uncontrollably by the time Camilla finished her cigarette and phone call. She sauntered in, expecting to hear Kelly gush about her boyfriend. Instead, she was horrified to see Kelly wracked with sobs.

"Kelly? What happened?" she asked in consternation. "Is it bad news from back in England?"

Kelly was much too ashamed at that moment to even tell anyone why she was crying. How could she admit to being the other woman – a home wrecker? The mere thought of it filled her with such intense self-loathing that she ran blindly out of the office, her tears streaming down her cheeks, blurring her vision. Camilla rushed off after her, not wanting to leave her alone in that state, but before she got to the stairs, she heard Kelly yell in pain. She had lost her footing and had fallen down the narrow, uneven stairs.

By the time Camilla reached the bottom, Kelly was huddled in a miserable heap, crying uncontrollably. "Kelly, darling. Are you hurt?

Can you stand up?" asked Camilla, trying to hoist Kelly up by taking her by the arm and levering Kelly up against her own body for support. But Kelly was determined to stay put on the floor, too miserable to get up.

Eventually, Camilla sat down beside her on the floor. She just waited for Kelly to cry it all out. Pulling a wad of tissues from her bag, which she had the good sense to grab on her way out, Camilla dabbed at Kelly's tear-streaked face gently and with the deepest compassion.

"Kelly, when you are ready to talk, I am here to listen to you, sweetheart. You don't have to deal with this alone, whatever it is. I am going to sit right here with you," vowed Camilla.

So, they sat in silence – punctuated now and then by Kelly blowing her nose between sobs. Eventually, her breath started to hitch, and she was slowly beginning to feel like she was all cried out.

"Camilla, I just found out that I am a home wrecker. I am a mistress – the other woman. A side dish!" she spat, disgusted.

"Oh. Is that all?" asked Camilla, relieved.

"What do you mean, 'Is that all?' Camilla? I have unwittingly ruined another woman's marriage. I am – I'm a slut!"

"Listen to me, cariña," said Camilla, taking Kelly firmly by the shoulders. "This guy knew exactly what he was doing. He chose to cheat on his wife with you. Did you entice him with your sexy outfits, high heels, and makeup? Did you stalk him and throw yourself at him until he had no choice but to date you? Come on, now. This is not your fault. You did not know he was married. Did he give you any reason to doubt him?"

"I will have to think about that. But it does explain why we never took our relationship to the next level. And he rarely stayed over. He was not thrilled when I arranged the New Year's holiday away and – come to think of it – he was totally relieved I had to cancel the trip and come to Spain instead! Oh, my gosh! I wonder if he has any children. I feel like such a monster right now, Camilla. Are you ashamed of me?"

"I'll tell you what I think. I think we should get off this floor, dust ourselves off, and go get some gelato. Come on. I am not taking no for an answer. Besides, a good sulk would not be complete without some ice cream to finish off the process. Let's go," commanded Camilla as she got up and then pulled Kelly up by the arms.

"I do love a good gelato, actually," admitted Kelly, sniffing, with the ghost of a smile playing on her pale face.

"Ah, now there is that left dimple I want to see. You are so pretty when you smile, Kelly darling. Don't let the likes of what's-his-name take that away from you. He is clearly a very unhappy man. I am just glad you found out about him now rather than later."

"You're right, Camilla. I need to bring myself to see this break-up as something positive. Ouch!"

"What's the matter, Kels?" asked Camilla, concerned.

"I think I twisted my ankle, but it isn't too bad. I think I need to just walk it off," said Kelly, wincing in pain but trying to put on a brave face.

"Alright, let's take it nice and slow. Lean on me as we walk until you feel stronger."

"Is the gelato place far away?"

"Not at all. It is just across the road from us, actually. How lucky are you, Kelly darling?" replied Camilla as she tried to take pressure off Kelly's injured ankle by supporting her as she stepped forward.

"Need some help?" asked an older Englishwoman, who stepped into their path, her tone friendly.

"Andie! How wonderful to see you." Camilla, slightly out of breath from helping Kelly walk, beamed as she recognised her. She leaned in to give the older woman – what Kelly now recognised as her signature – air kisses on each cheek and a fierce hug.

"Andie, I'd like you to meet Judy's niece, Kelly. Kelly, meet Andie – an old friend to both Judy and me. Andie is ex-MI6 – so we need not have any fear when she is around, right, Andie?" teased Camilla with a wink. A good giggle from everyone followed that.

"It is wonderful to meet you, Andie. You were friends with Aunt Judy. I would love to hear stories about her time with you all here in Lubrín. She seldom talked much about her life over here," explained Kelly, intrigued by Andie – and grateful for the distraction.

"I have a marvellously delicious idea. Andie darling, if you are not too busy, would you like to join us for some gelato?" asked Camilla hopefully.

"I would love to," replied Andie, as her sleek grey hair wafted about her face in the breeze. "I am kind of helping with an ongoing investigation, but I could spare a few moments to catch up with old and new friends." Her grey eyes flashed with emerald flecks as they gleamed with amusement at the prospect of having a bit of fun.

"Wonderful, mi amiga! It will be my treat, dear chiquitas," exclaimed Camilla gleefully. And the odd trio set off for the ice cream parlour.

3

The Road Trip

"I really think that we should tell her the truth, Camilla," hissed Andie in a loud whisper. "Forewarned is forearmed, you know. She is in a strange land, populated by locals who can't help being suspicious of an Englishwoman whom they will always distrust," she implored further.

"Judy was very clear about this, Andie. She placed you on protection detail from the moment Kelly set foot on Spanish soil. But discretion and secrecy are not negotiable. That was the contract, and you agreed to it!" countered Camilla in an equally vehement hiss.

"Yes, but that was before all these crimes started happening around Lubrín and the surrounding areas, Camilla. They are stealing ancient artefacts only. These rare pieces have been passed down the family trees of the most ancient families in Spain. She has to know the truth so she can take added precautions. We aren't always going to be there to protect her at every moment. Come on, let's be practical about this. I mean, she doesn't even know the truth about who she is!" persisted Andie.

"Here she comes. Let's discuss this later," replied Camilla, flashing an enormous smile as Kelly approached Andie's zippy white Audi A5.

Kelly wore soft, baggy olive-green corduroy trousers with an oversized cream-coloured jacket that made Camilla cringe. Luckily, the ensemble was saved by a beautiful green and scarlet scarf interspersed with gold details, which she wore haphazardly around her neck. A crochet cross-body bag and comfy brown hush puppies completed the look. Of course, the emerald cat-eye spectacles were a permanent part of Kelly's charm.

I have got to make time to take this woman shopping, thought Camilla ruefully. But she knew that Kelly's self-confidence was at an all-time low, so she said, "Ah, Kelly. You look like a breath of fresh air. Are you excited about our sightseeing trip?"

"Hi, ladies. I sure am. There is nothing like a good tour to spice up the weekend," she replied, not wanting to put a damper on the day out. But the telltale dark circles underneath her eyes gave away the fact that she had been up all night crying into her pillow.

It had all been too much for her, and she couldn't pick up the phone and find Aunt Judy's warm, loving voice on the other end of the line. As much as she loved travelling to faraway destinations, Kelly somehow felt like she was up the creek without a paddle out in Spain. Of course, Camilla was a huge help – with everything. But the language barrier, unfriendly employees and clients, and having to adjust to all the bureaucratic red tape involved in land sales and acquisitions, was proving to be a bit too much to handle on the work front.

Personally, her abandonment issues had frayed her nerves, as Lenny was only able to make a trip out to Spain in the next two weeks at the earliest. He and Laura would try to make it for the Bread Festival and then go on a week-long cycling holiday in Lubrín and the surrounding areas.

Lenny worked for Laura's father as the company's CEO, and he had the freedom to take at least one cycling holiday per month as long as he included some networking and business expansion into his itinerary. They were a popular brand that specialised in designing and manufacturing sports and fitness equipment, including those used in extreme sports. So Lenny was able to feed his cycling addiction by working it into his sales pitches and business trips. Unfortunately for Kelly, that meant that she had to contend with long stretches of silence when he was on the road because he seldom called or emailed while he was on tour.

And then there was the fresh break-up that had ripped her heart to shreds and made her question her own integrity and self-worth. She was grateful for Andie and Camilla, who refused to let her mope about Judy's old flat, which she had moved into. If it were up to her, Kelly would have spent the weekend working on crosswords and ciphers, dressed in her pyjamas.

"First, we shall have breakfast at our local coffee shop bakery. Señora Alba's tortilla española is the best way to start this sort of day," gushed Camilla as she performed her usual shoulder shuffle whenever she talked about anything she enjoyed.

"I'm kinda partial to her croquetas de jamón myself," added Andie dreamily.

"How are her mejillones rellenos?" asked Kelly, trying to sound like she had learned something in the two weeks she had been in Spain.

"Oh, that sounds like the perfect addition to our dinner menu when we get to the coast. It will go perfectly with the seafood paella I have my heart set on when we get to the beach at Almería," Camilla gushed.

Kelly wondered how Camilla managed to stay in such great shape despite her love for food and wine.

"Ah, Señora Alba," tittered Camilla as she swooshed into the bakery with the chic clickety-clack of her stiletto heels drawing attention to their grand entrance, as if her black and white polka-dotted dress wouldn't adequately do the trick.

"You know Andie Spears, of course. And this is Kelly Simpson." Camilla spoke in English for Kelly's benefit, and then, responding to the blank uncomprehending expression Señora Alba wore, she continued to speak rapidly in Spanish until understanding finally dawned on the middle-aged woman's face.

She was the epitome of grace and hospitality thereafter, and the Spanish breakfast omelette was the most hearty breakfast Kelly had eaten in a very long time. But Kelly could not shake the uncomfortable feeling that she was being watched despite the jovial atmosphere of the little bakery-cum-coffee shop.

Before setting off on their outing, Kelly thought she would use the ladies' room. In a dark, recessed booth near the bathroom sat a strange-looking old man she had met once before. She recalled that first meeting with him a few days after Aunt Judy's funeral. It was on January 5, to be precise, during the festival of the Three Kings. Kelly had been walking around that evening, taking advantage of the busy pedestrian traffic to clear her head in the safety of the crowd. There was a little parade, and the children were shrieking with joy, collecting sweets thrown from the floats. Amidst the revelry, Kelly skulked along on the periphery, carefully stepping over the children's shoes that had been placed outside the doorways of each house. She later learned that these would be filled with little trinkets and presents by morning.

Suddenly, out of a dark alley emerged that same old, bent-over man with wrinkles and ancient scars on his face. "*Su tía fue asesinada,*" he said urgently as he grabbed her arm. He repeated those words in a foreboding tone before melting into the thronging crowd. Kelly had been dazed and quite out of it at the time. Her ears had not quite adapted to hearing Spanish, especially when spoken in the local dialect, so she could not make any sense of what the strange man had been trying to tell her. But she soon forgot about the incident and immersed herself in learning everything there was to learn about running an estate agency in Spain.

But she recognised the man instantly at Señora Alba's coffee shop that morning. With his gnarled, knotted fingers, he grabbed Kelly's arm again as she passed and whispered almost inaudibly, "Está en peligro. Ellos le están buscando." Kelly felt a cold chill run down her spine at the ominous tone in which he had spoken. But, again, she could not make sense of what he had said to her. She managed to break free and dive into the bathroom. By the time she hazarded a peek outside the washroom, the strange man had gone and nobody had seen him there in the first place.

"I wish I had understood what he was saying. It seemed to be very important," wailed Kelly. She told Camilla and Andie about the festival of the Three Kings and tried to repeat what he had told her on both occasions. They simply exchanged meaningful glances and then laughed at Kelly's attempt at speaking Spanish. But not before Kelly had picked up on the worried vibe between the two older women. She chose to keep silent – not wanting to ruin their day out – but she vowed to get to the bottom of it by herself somehow.

Andie played tour guide as they drove along and Camilla played the jester to try to diffuse the bad taste the incident had left in their mouths. "Did you know that Lubrín's history can be traced as far back as three-and-a-half million years? Yep, early man left darkest Africa and found his way into the Almanzora Valley. We're now heading to a place called the Bat Cave on the way to El Marchal, where we shall see the carvings on the Wax Stones in El Campico."

"You'd better sit back and enjoy the ride, Kelly darling. It is about three hours away. But the landscape along the way is breathtaking," added Camilla, almost apologetically.

"Sounds like fun. Thanks for doing this, you two. I appreciate you taking the time out to play tour guide to the likes of me," said Kelly.

Camilla insisted that they stop at Granada for a bit of a shopping spree at the Moroccan souk. While Kelly was preoccupied with the beautiful hand-crafted goods in the colourful market stalls, Camilla and Andie discussed the strange old man's warnings to Kelly.

"The first time she met him, he told her that Judy had been murdered! Murdered, Andie!" Camilla was finally relieved to be able to voice the terror she had been trying to keep from Kelly. "You always suspected foul play, Andie, and that old man confirmed it. Thank goodness Kelly didn't understand what he'd said. But she is learning, and it is only a matter of time before she gets it," continued Camilla, chewing nervously on a perfectly manicured nail. They stood outside a shoe stall where she had bought a pair of black trainers for the hike to the cave.

"My biggest concern right now is the second warning he gave her – from this morning. He said that she is in grave danger and that they are looking for her," admitted Andie, looking around furtively – an old habit that had saved her more times than she cared to remember.

"What do you think?" asked Kelly, holding up a chunky cardigan several sizes too big for her. Camilla simply rolled her eyes and groaned dramatically, while the other two women laughed heartily.

While in the city, they made a quick visit to the Granada Cathedral and the lookout point to view the Alhambra Palace before grabbing some delicious Moroccan tea at one of the more decadent tea shops in the area. Kelly marvelled at the Spanish and Moorish influences in the architectural and decor elements, not to mention the delicious flavour profiles created by this unique fusion of cultures in the realm of gastronomy.

After vowing to revisit Granada, the trio headed for the Bat Cave. They enjoyed a light picnic along the scenic return journey toward Almería and spent what was left of the afternoon on the beach. Dinner was a seafood feast paired with a light white wine that left the women completely satiated. They got back to Lubrín at around 10:30 p.m. to find the town buzzing with activity outside Kelly's flat despite the severe drop in temperature.

"Inspector Gamero, what is going on here?" asked Andie, instinctively taking charge.

"Good evening, Señora Spears. The neighbours caught sight of a cat burglar who allegedly tried to gain entry into the late Señora Fargo's flat. But the perpetrator disappeared into the night once they were discovered," reported Inspector Gamero in his usual bored tone. A cloud of mist floated out of his mouth like an apparition in the chilly darkness.

"That is just awful! Thank goodness you weren't at home, Kelly," said Camilla, grabbing Kelly by her arms. "That settles it. You are spending the rest of the weekend with me. I don't want to hear another word about it."

"I-I am sure I will be okay. I don't want to impose on you."

"Perhaps you should bunk with Camilla until we can get to the bottom of this, Kelly," advised Andie. "I will work closely with Gamero on this. No doubt it is part of the syndicate that has been creating a nuisance in a spate of thefts all over Lubrín in recent weeks."

Kelly thanked the neighbours, who still eyed her with the utmost suspicion. The husband simply gave her a nod, turned on his heels, and went back into his house, followed by his wife, who at least gave her a compassionate smile but also said nothing.

After verifying that nothing was amiss in the flat, Kelly packed a bag, grateful to Camilla for offering to have a sleepover. “This will be fun. You’ll see, Kelly darling,” assured Camilla, giving Kelly’s shoulders a good squeeze.

4

The Sisterhood

"Okay, but have you ever dated more than one guy at a time?" asked Kelly, mischievously – with the dessert spoon still wedged between her teeth.

"Hmm," mused Camilla, thoughtfully. "I think my record for the number of men I've dated all at once was four," she concluded, nodding her head in confirmation.

"What! No, way! How did you manage to find time to date them all? That couldn't have ended well!" It seemed inconceivable to Kelly that anyone could ever have that much time and energy to devote to multiple romantic interests at once.

Camilla laughed throatily at the recollection. "Actually, two of them were a father and stepson and I didn't know it until the jig was up!"

"No! Camilla! That's outrageous!" shrieked Kelly, more than a little mortified at the idea.

They were a few hours into a good old bonding session, complete with multiple outfit changes, makeup, makeovers, and, of course, loads of ice cream and an assortment of junk food. Kelly was not really into all the clothes and makeup, but she appreciated Camilla's efforts to take her mind off things. So she pushed aside her fears and lost herself in the moment. The thought that someone had tried to gain entry into Aunt Judy's flat had set Kelly on edge. A nagging sense of being kept out of the loop had also begun to creep into Kelly's mind, merely on an instinctive level for the time being. She just couldn't shake the feeling that all was not what it seemed.

Nevertheless, they laughed until their sides hurt and tears streamed down their faces. Of course, no female bonding session would be complete if there weren't at least a few teary confessions, shared secrets, and a delve into their heaps of regrets.

Before they knew it, the sky had turned from inky to grey, and the cocks had begun to announce the dawn's imminent arrival.

"Shoot, we've been up all night. I can't believe it," said Kelly in wonderment.

"I think I am gonna hit the shower and then the bed, Kelly darling," decided Camilla groggily. She had added liquor to her ice cream and the combination was not sitting well in her tummy. She stumbled toward the bathroom and slammed the door shut behind her.

Kelly heard the sound of retching from the other side. "Camilla? Are you alright, hun?" asked Kelly, caught between trying to be serious and wanting to giggle.

"I... I'm alright. I just need a few minutes. Don't worry about me."

"Okay. Shout if you need anything," called Kelly at the bathroom door.

While Camilla was in the bathroom, preoccupied with the effects of the copious amount of alcohol she had been drinking to steady her nerves, Kelly thought she would have a look around. Pushing up her emerald cat-eyed spectacles until they straddled the bridge of her nose, she took a closer look at Camilla's ornate bookshelf, which seemed to contain an impressive assortment of titles. There was a laudable selection of first editions ensconced in a protective glass casing. On the opposite end, Kelly noticed an ancient copy of Robert Louis

Stevenson's Treasure Island that had been placed upside down at the far end of the middle shelf. It struck Kelly as rather odd, considering how immaculately Camilla's home was organised without the slightest thing out of place.

Kelly assumed that perhaps one of Camilla's lovers may have absent-mindedly pawed through her book collection while waiting for her to emerge from the bathroom – much like what she was doing at that moment herself – and they simply hadn't bothered to replace it the right way up. Kelly tugged at the book, to reorient it, when, to her astonishment, the book turned out to be a lever that opened up a small rectangular recess in the wall. Just then, Kelly's mind felt a twinge of guilt about snooping around until Judy's name caught her eye in the half-light of the little study.

Tossing aside the feeling that she was snooping, Kelly rationalised that her need for answers about her aunt trumped all other considerations. Judy's name, in her aunt's own elegant script, was written on an envelope – the kind that Kelly remembered awaiting with great anticipation throughout her teenage years, as they invariably contained a loving message and some sort of puzzle, cipher, or code as a treat. Kelly had no doubt that the envelope contained a message from Aunt Judy as it was her aunt's stationery, and the hunger for any sort of contact with her late aunt spurred her on despite the obvious invasion of privacy she knew she was committing.

Beside the envelope was a midnight blue velvet jewellery bag. Since I am snooping anyway, I may as well be thorough about it, she reasoned to herself wryly as she poured the contents of the bag gently into the palm of her hand. A heavy, intricately worked chain and pendant shimmered and sparkled in her hand. It was obviously some sort of heirloom, and if it had belonged to Aunt Judy, perhaps she had bequeathed it to Camilla. Kelly felt a pang of envy at the notion that Judy would give such a personal and obviously valuable family heirloom to someone else. Nevertheless, she took a closer look at the piece. The links of the chain seemed to interlock into a sort of thick rope with intricate patterns around it while the pendant was encrusted with a variety of precious and semi-precious stones – the work was fine and fussy. In the centre of the pendant was a black sapphire. Kelly had never seen anything like it. Turning to the reverse side, Kelly noticed an inscription in an ancient script – Aztec perhaps. It also had some sort of mystical symbol inscribed on it. It looked like runes of some sort.

Kelly proceeded to read the contents of the letter. It read:

Dear Camilla,

If you are reading this, it means that I am no longer around to protect the family heritage, which means that the package is in peril from those bent on destroying the work of generations of our family.

Kelly is to be eased into her new responsibilities, and I am entrusting her into your care, my faithful friend. Between you and Andie Spears, I have every confidence that you will succeed. Should it be necessary, Lenny should be apprised of the status and level of risk. He will know what to do.

I have enclosed a catalogue of the artefacts in chronological order and the generation to which they belonged. You know where they are housed and Kelly, when she is ready, will take over custodianship of the property and its contents.

Please protect the package from all who seek to destroy it. Thank you for your dedicated service to the cause that was thrust upon you. It has been my utmost privilege to have been surrounded by women of substance like you and Andie. It is my fervent wish that Kelly is prepared for the responsibilities that lie ahead of her.

With love and gratitude,

JF

Kelly's vision blurred as unbidden tears cascaded down her cheeks. The floodgates of grief were flung open, and she finally mourned her late aunt without reservation. Confusion and grief competed for attention in her mind. Why was she excluded – not her inner circle? And who was her Aunt Judy, really? She vaguely took notice of the second sheet of paper, which contained the catalogue of artefacts.

"Kelly," gasped Camilla, who stood aghast in her towel, surrounded by an aura of steam like some sort of superheroine.

"What is this, Camilla? When were you planning to tell me? What is going on? I, I need answers!" Kelly's voice had started off soft – barely a whisper – but had crescendoed until she shrieked out the last words in exasperation.

"Kelly, there is much that we have to discuss but not until you are ready." Camilla's tone was in direct contrast to Kelly's shriek, as if to soothe her.

"When were you going to tell me the truth, Camilla? I trusted you! And – and Aunt Judy trusted you. But you have been giving me the run-around. Why?" implored Kelly, her eyes conveying betrayal.

"There are things that I am not at liberty to tell you just yet. For your own safety. I swore to protect you at all costs, and that is what I intend to do."

"What danger? What are you talking about? You're not making any sense! You wanna know what I think, Camilla? I think you just want to keep all of Aunt Judy's heirlooms and artefacts to yourself!" In her fit of rage and grief, Kelly lashed out viciously.

"I know that you're upset. There are things that I just cannot tell you just yet. But I will! Believe me, I will. When you're ready. But for now, I need you to trust me, Kelly. Do you think you could do that, please?" implored Camilla, kneeling before Kelly, who had collapsed in a heap at the edge of the bed.

"You make it sound like I have a choice."

"Oh, come here," consoled Camilla, enveloping Kelly in her arms. "It will all make sense to you soon, Kelly darling. I promise you this. But if Aunt Judy trusted me with this, don't you think that you can as well?" asked Camilla, her eyes looking searchingly into Kelly's teary ones.

"I will have to think about it, Camilla. I don't know. I just don't know," answered Kelly frankly.

"That sounds fair. How about you hop in the shower and then sleep on it?"

The second Camilla heard the shower tap turn on, she got hold of Andie. "She found the catalogue and knows that there are things we haven't told her. We need to tread even more cautiously from now on. Right. Tomorrow."

Kelly knew that Camilla would use the time she was in the shower to call someone, so she eavesdropped on the conversation; for all the good it did her. There was only one thing to do, she decided. She would go over to Aunt Judy's property in the country alone and without telling anyone. She would get to the bottom of all the cloak and dagger stuff – once and for all.

5

Shadow Work

It didn't take much digging for Kelly to find the address to Aunt Judy's country villa, *Casa del la Duradera* meaning, "House of the Enduring." Pleading a headache, she left Camilla's the next day, taking the catalogue list and heirloom along with her. There was no protest from Camilla, who understood that Kelly needed time to process everything that had happened. For her part, Camilla also needed time to intensify the plan already in place to safeguard Kelly at all times.

It was late afternoon by the time Kelly got back to the flat, but she was determined not to waste another moment. So, she packed a fresh set of clothes, deciding to spend the night at *Casa del la Duradera* and return to town early on Monday, before she would be missed.

The drive out to the country was just what she needed to clear her mind. There was just something about the undulant roads and dry natural scenery that helped Kelly unwind. The villa was more than an hour from Lubrín, seemingly in the middle of nowhere without another house in sight for miles, but Kelly welcomed the isolation.

The sun was already setting by the time Kelly had pulled up to the colossal mansion that seemed to be drenched in the last echoes of sunset, which was also the colour of the *casa* with white trimmings and balconies providing some relief from the monochromatic edifice. The mansion was structured on three terraced levels, hugging the gradient of the land. Delightfully gurgling water from the water feature at the centre of the driveway filled the crisp evening air with a musicality that seemed to bring the entire place to life. A decorative, well-loved garden consisting of a rockery, shrubs, and trees added a fantastical charm to the place with thoughtful little touches like bird feeders and baths, a garden bench or two, and bamboo wind chimes that hung from one of the taller trees. Intricate mosaic artwork surrounded the water fountain that created a sophisticated roundabout, which was completed by a perfectly manicured hedge around its circumference. *Now, I could live in a place like this,* thought Kelly, taking in a huge gulp of the crisp evening air.

As her eyes soaked in the beauty of her surroundings, a nondescript SUV without plates and dark-tinted windows caught Kelly's eye. It was parked in the shadows at the far end of the main building. *Now, this looks like trouble,* thought Kelly as her heart began to race. *I am not taking any chances after what happened at the flat. I bet the Casa del la Duradera is filled with ancient artefacts—just what the criminals seem to be after.*

Deciding to lock her overnight bag in the car, she hauled out a can of pepper spray from her purse. *Boy, am I glad I listened to Lenny and got this the day I landed in Spain. I wish you were here right now, bro,* she thought with a pang of longing.

Pushing on, she made her way stealthily to the entrance of the villa to find that the door had been prised open and the alarm system forcefully deactivated—there were wires sticking out of the control panel and a low, frantic beeping sound emanated from the panel. *Time to call in the cavalry, I think,* thought Kelly, hauling out her mobile phone. She texted Andie and Camilla rapidly, sending them a location pin of where she was before switching off her phone to not disturb the intruder.

Kelly could hear the faint sounds coming from upstairs. Grabbing a poker from the fireplace, she gingerly tiptoed her way up the tiled staircase with her back against the wall. Once on the landing, she noticed the oscillating beam of a flashlight coming from a room at the end of the hall. Despite her deafening elevated heart rate, Kelly bravely edged toward danger.

Suddenly, a loud clang echoed through the house as a large metal object hit the marble floor. *"Mierda!"* grunted the thick voice of the intruder. His voice sent chills down Kelly's spine.

You are in way over your head here, Kelly girl, she told herself as she felt a bead of icy sweat run down her spine.

Kelly's nerves went into overdrive as her palms became so sweaty that she could scarcely hold on to the heavy poker. Her breathing grew ragged, and she struggled to regain normal breath control. *Well, we are here now. There's nothing for it but to face this guy. No way am I letting him take any of Aunt Judy's things!*

Reaching the heavy oak door at the end of the hall, Kelly raised the poker, ready to strike. Hazarding a peek into what seemed to be a little museum, she was completely astounded by the treasures on display. *Had to hand it to Aunt Judy to have a museum in her country mansion,* thought Kelly wryly, pushing her glasses up the bridge of her nose.

A sudden movement caught her eye in the far corner of the room. The burglar was a thickset man of medium height, clad in a black polo neck sweater that seemed to be a few sizes too small for his bulky upper body. He wore black joggers and black trainers. The balaclava over his face made it impossible for Kelly to distinguish any of his features. *Anyway, his back is turned, thank goodness,* observed Kelly as she crept into the room and crouched behind a display pillar. *If I survive this and he gets away, I will need to give the police as much info as possible,* she reasoned as she tried to get a better look at the man.

Chalking up her bravery to the adrenaline rush and a delayed nervous response due to the alcohol consumption of the previous night, she slunk her way around the room unnoticed. The intruder was rummaging intently through a collection of ancient artefacts in various cases within a cupboard in one of the two islands in the room. *How dare he paw through Aunt Judy's things like that!* Outrage trumped fear as Kelly felt the bile rise in her throat at the thought of this brazen violation.

Navigating her way behind the low pillars upon which stood an assortment of busts and displays around the octagonal room, she crept stealthily toward the burglar. Managing to get up behind him undetected, Kelly unfurled her body to its full height.

Here goes nothing. Her hands trembled as she raised the poker above her head, poised to strike.

Unfortunately, the burglar's eye caught sight of her shadow on the wall in front of them – his lightning-fast reflexes allowing her no chance to strike. He wheeled around and held her in a vice-like grip in one fluid motion. Dropping his torch, he grabbed the poker with his other hand.

"Mierda!" he repeated for the second time, as the poker crashed to the floor, dashing Kelly's hopes of making it through this alive. He grunted unintelligibly in Spanish as he squeezed on Kelly's vagus nerve. Her nostrils were assaulted by the pungent odour of sweat and tobacco as he pinned her back against him, breathing heavily with exertion.

In a valiant attempt at breaking free, Kelly tried to use her heels to kick him in the shins and her elbows to sucker-punch him in the diaphragm. But he anticipated her every move, countering them like she were a petulant child – he mocked her menacingly – and increased the pressure on her neck.

Don't pass out! Don't pass out! But it was futile – her vision blurred and she slipped away, not before the wailing of sirens in the distance announced the arrival of local law enforcement.

I knew they would come through, thought Kelly, before passing out completely.

"Señora Simpson, wake up. Señora Simpson, can you hear me?" The voice sounded miles away, at first, but Kelly came to gradually. Her eyes fluttered open and she looked around groggily. Suddenly, it all came flooding back to her, and she sat bolt upright on the floor. "Did you get him?" she asked frantically.

"Bicho malo nunca muere!" replied the matronly-looking paramedic with a sigh. And then, in response to Kelly's confused expression, she added, "It means a bad bug never dies. No, Señora, the perpetrator got away. But the police will track down that *cabròn*. Have no fear." The pleasant attendant gave Kelly's arm a reassuring squeeze. "Let us focus on you, *sí*?"

While the paramedic conducted her examination, a rather attractive man approached Kelly. Feeling somewhat self-conscious in that state, Kelly wished she'd had a sliver of Camilla's grace and elegance at that moment.

"Señora Simpson. How do you feel?" he asked. Concern had turned his honey-coloured eyes dreamy. Kelly whimpered involuntarily and hoped he hadn't heard her. But his knowing smile said otherwise, and Kelly felt like her cheeks were on fire.

"I am Inspector Ignacio Vargas, and I have been working with our local precincts on the stolen artefact cases. We have reason to believe that it is the work of a syndicate whose base of operations is in Lubrín. Would you be able to tell us if anything is missing from Señora Fargo's impressive collection here?"

"I... I have a catalogue in my bag. It's in my car," offered Kelly, trying to get up.

"Would you care to tell me what you are doing out here by yourself at this time of the day, Señora?" he pressed on.

Mild outrage at having to account for why she was on the property that was technically hers propelled Kelly into action. "Are you seriously going to stand around interrogating the victim when the criminal who broke the law is still at large? I must say that the law enforcement here is a joke!" Kelly's tone was bitter.

"Kelly darling!" cried a familiar voice, which was followed by the staccato sound of Camilla's rapidly approaching heels. "Are you alright? Did that *puto* hurt you?" she asked, fussing over Kelly like a mother hen.

"I'm alright. But instead of hunting him down, this detective is wasting precious time interrogating me."

"Ignacio." Camilla nodded, folding her arms and turning away from him.

"Camilla," he replied, equally coolly.

"Oh, great! So you two used to be lovers!" observed Kelly, rolling her eyes.

"Water under the bridge," dismissed the inspector.

"I barely recall. So, it can't have been that riveting," retorted Camilla off-handedly.

"They say that the memory is the first to go. Pity!" he continued, obviously goading her further.

The torrent of Spanish that followed, along with the impassioned body language, told Kelly that they were going to be of little help. So she got up carefully and made her way to the car, where she retrieved the catalogue list.

She went through every artefact on the list, ensuring that it was in fact in its rightful place – all save one, an ancient puzzle box with gold inlay details.

"Inspector Vargas. I have done a thorough check, and it seems like only one item is missing from the collection. I can't say for certain that he took it, but it is an ancient gold-inlaid puzzle box," reported Kelly.

"Very well. We will add it to the list of pilfered items. This rabble has managed to amass a sizeable pile of treasures from the ancient families they have targeted. But rest assured, Señora Simpson, the net is closing in on them."

"Ignacio!" greeted Andie. "Kelly! Are you alright? What possessed you to come out here by yourself in the dark?" scolded Andie after giving Kelly a warm hug.

"I just wanted to catalogue Aunt Judy's artefacts and have a look around. I am actually glad I managed to scare off the burglar. Who knows what else he would have made off with had I not been here? I shudder to think what would have happened if you hadn't sent the cops to check on the place, Andie."

"I am just glad that you are alright. Promise me that you are going to behave yourself from now on, or I am going to have to put a guard detail on you twenty-four-seven. I hope I've made myself clear!"

Kelly saluted with a groggy, "Ma'am. Yes, ma'am!"

"Ignacio, a word, if you please?" Andie and Inspector Ignacio Vargas had a long chat outside. Meanwhile, an armed officer escorted Kelly and Camilla home for some much-needed rest.

6

The Bloody Tour

In the wake of their harrowing yet eventful weekend, the prospect of facing what seemed like a month of Mondays at the office was proving rather daunting for Kelly and Camilla alike.

Although she hated to admit it, Kelly was growing addicted to living on the edge. She had certainly experienced more excitement than she had bargained for in the short time she had lived in the usually sleepy town of Lubrín. And the endless dunes of dry paperwork awaiting her attention at the office threatened to send her into a tailspin for the foreseeable future. She would have preferred to spend her time investigating the stolen artefacts and getting to the bottom of why and how Aunt Judy was somehow one of the targets.

The unsettling notion that perhaps Aunt Judy may have been murdered was becoming a not-so-far-fetched, growing possibility. Kelly kept trying to remember the exact words the old man had told her so that she could punch them into her translator app. It seemed like he had told her that her relative had been murdered and she was in danger. Unfortunately, she would have to resume her digging some other time.

Her immediate concern was the tricky issue of a seller who had failed to settle his land tax by the end of June the previous year and insisted on being exempt. Kelly had to wade through all the conditions stipulated in Modelo 714 with regards to the local land rates commonly called *Impuesto sobre Bienes Inmuebles* or IBI. This was the annual land tax based on the cadastral value of the property. To compound matters, the property was being purchased by a UK citizen who had failed to secure an NIE number—the identification number for foreigners in Spain. Foreigners who wish to purchase property and conduct any other legal business in the country could only do so if they were in possession of this magic number. Unfortunately, the folks at the local *Oficina de Extranjerìa* or "Legalisation Office" were reluctant to assist. Kelly suspected that a bit of palm greasing would do the trick.

After spending two days poring over the intricacies of land acquisition by a foreigner, Kelly was ready to tear her hair out in frustration. "You know what you need, Kelly darling? A break. What do you say we ditch the office and take an extended lunch? I could do with a spot of sightseeing around town myself. What do you think?"

"I don't know," replied Kelly. "Do tapas and gelato come with this offer?" They smiled, once more in cahoots with each other.

"But of course. I should have led with that. *Vámonos!*" Camilla commanded gleefully, pulling out her phone to invite Andie to join them.

"I think we shall visit Our Lady of the Rosary Church. It is near a restaurant I've been meaning to take Kelly to and we can grab a gelato on our way back to the office. What do you say, Andie?"

With all the arrangements made, the trio met twenty minutes later at the quaint little café bar across from the church. "I can't shake the feeling that Aunt Judy was murdered," confessed Kelly helplessly.

"Well, I studied the autopsy report and chatted with the old man who discovered her body," began Andie, looking around furtively before leaning in. "But I have to admit that we cannot discount the possibility. The autopsy did reveal a few discrepancies," she confessed in a low whisper.

"Like what? Why didn't you tell me any of this before?" hissed Kelly, somewhat put out by Andie's reluctance.

"The matter is still under investigation. I didn't want to say anything until I was confident about what really happened to Judy. And I will thank you for not interfering either, Kelly Simpson. I am warning you. We don't know who we are dealing with or what Judy got herself mixed up in—"

"It is preposterous to think that Aunt Judy would do anything illegal or support thugs and gangsters. Whoever did this must have caught her completely unawares," interrupted Kelly, her loyalty fierce.

"Well," Camilla interjected. "I have every confidence that the authorities are doing their best to get to the bottom of it. But I think that they will have a better chance if we keep quiet about the investigation and not create too many waves in this tiny town. It will send the criminals into the hills, or completely underground," she explained rationally.

"I think we should get going on the tour aspect of our afternoon plans before we work ourselves into a frenzy," suggested Andie.

"I suppose it is important to keep up appearances."

"The church was actually built quite recently. It was commissioned by Bishop José María Orbera in 1880 and stands in honour of Our Lady of the Rosary. The congregation is shared with Saint Sebastian in the town," began Camilla, with her most professional tour guide impression.

"Notice the modern nineteenth-century touches of red brick and iron, features you will be hard-pressed to find at any of the older churches in Spain," supplied Andie, not to be outdone by Camilla. "The architecture is typical nineteenth-century with a Latin cross plan and three naves—" she continued but was interrupted by a loud and terrifying scream that rang out eerily from the back of the church.

By the time they got to the source of the scream, there was already a sizeable crowd gathered around a recessed, closed entrance behind the church.

"Wait here," instructed Andie, moving forward into the little gathering.

Speaking in Spanish and English, Andie instructed everyone to file into the church immediately. She got on the phone at once. As the crowd thinned around the recessed entrance, Kelly and Camilla finally saw what the commotion was about. A body lay sprawled on the floor against the right wall. His clothes were drenched in blood, and he looked dead. Around him were scattered artefacts and an expensive-looking large metal case that seemed to have housed them mere moments ago.

Inspector Vargas and his partner, Adán Gamero, got to the church within minutes. Taking full control over the crime scene, they ordered their team to detain everyone who had been at the scene when the crime was committed. Interrogations and statements would continue until everyone's account of events had been documented.

"Camilla," whispered Kelly. "Look!" She nodded in the direction of the spilled artefacts. "Over there," she insisted. But Camilla did not understand what she was trying to say.

"It's the puzzle box! The dead guy must be the burglar I caught at Aunt Judy's villa!" hissed Kelly.

"Are you sure?"

"I am going in for a closer look. Keep an eye out for the police." She winked and sneaked off toward the artefacts.

"That's a bad idea, Kelly! Kelly!" called Camilla frantically in a whispered shriek. But Kelly was long gone.

The body had been dispatched to the coroner's office, and the forensics team was systematically gathering evidence around the crime scene. They seemed too engrossed in their work to notice Kelly pick up the puzzle box. Turning over the ivory and gold-inlaid puzzle box, she noticed that it also contained the two symbols she had seen on the back of Aunt Judy's pendant. It looked like a ripple made with three concentric rings and what looked like an ancient battleaxe beside it.

Through excited curiosity, Kelly shook the box a couple of times and tapped it, managing to solve the puzzle in a trice. Without warning, a secret panel of the puzzle box gave way. Nestled within the blue velvet-coated compartment of the box was a strip of ancient cloth with a message scrawled on it in an elegant deep indigo archaic script. It was in Spanish, so Kelly gingerly hauled out her phone and snapped off a few quick pics of the symbols and message.

"Hey, what are you doing here?" asked one of the forensic scientists near her. Carefully pocketing the message, Kelly closed the puzzle box and replaced it on the floor discreetly. She noticed that a tiny jewel box that had turned over on its side also carried the same symbols. But she got what she needed and apologised in her most Camilla-esque tone, *"Lo siento."* She smiled sweetly, putting her palms up to show that she hadn't taken anything. Backing away with that same sweet smile, despite the aggrieved expression and tone of the scientist who caught her, she made her way back to Camilla.

"Kelly, you are incorrigible!" scolded Camilla.

"Sorry, Mummy," retorted Kelly, hardly able to contain her excitement. "It *was* Aunt Judy's puzzle box. So, this man must have been here to meet a buyer or something. He was clearly trying to fence the goods he'd stolen."

"Be that as it may, Kelly, you should not have gone snooping. We don't yet know what type of people we're dealing with or how extensive their organisation is."

"You make a valid point," mused Kelly. "Oh, and by the way, I managed to open the puzzle box," she announced grandly. Camilla was intrigued despite her fears.

"Look what I found inside," whispered Kelly, carefully showing Camilla the pictures she had taken with her phone.

"And look – these two symbols are etched into every artefact he stole. That must indicate that they belonged to the same collection or were made by the same company or something like that!" Kelly could hardly contain her excitement now.

"Good sleuthing, Kelly. But I wish you would be careful. We don't yet know what we're up against here," cautioned Camilla, despite her obvious admiration for Kelly's keen skills.

Andie came over to check in on them and, in a lowered tone, gave them a little update on what the authorities had managed to uncover.

"It seems like a couple of tourists who are just passing through Lubrín on their way down to the beach stumbled upon a nefarious transaction involving the deceased and his killer. The young German girl and her father disturbed the murderer who had just delivered the lethal jab, right in the heart, and was trying to pry the case out of his hands. He fled the scene when the witnesses arrived. The metal case opened in the fray, spilling its contents, and the offender was forced to flee without his booty," she surmised.

"How are you two holding up?" she continued, looking from one to the other, picking up on the undercurrent of elation they were struggling to contain.

"It turns out that we have an intrepid sleuth in our midst, Andie."

Kelly and Camilla filled Andie in on what Kelly had discovered. Kelly judiciously omitted the fact that she had swiped evidence. She kept the piece of cloth she'd pinched from the puzzle box safely tucked away in her trouser pocket.

"Great work, Kelly. But in the interests of safety, I will thank you to leave the sleuthing to the trained professionals, please. I think that Judy would be turning in her grave with horror at how much danger you've already encountered here. She would not be pleased with us, her dearest friends, for not keeping you safe. I'm afraid we've failed her," admitted Andie, looking dejectedly on the ground, drawing invisible semicircles on the cobbled-stoned path with the tip of her boot.

"Oh, come now. I am a grown woman of thirty-six! You can hardly be expected to keep me in check. But I promise to tread cautiously in future," she added sweetly, in response to Andie's warning look.

Back in the safety of her flat, Kelly carefully took the ancient piece of cloth out of her pocket and placed it in a clean plastic ziplock bag. She thereafter copied out the inscription into her notebook. And, feeding the message into her translator app despite the ancient dialect of the text, she waited impatiently for the search engine to work. After what seemed like several minutes had passed, she groaned in frustration when the search turned up empty. "I might have known this was going to be a challenge to figure out," she muttered.

Locking the evidence away in her bedside table drawer, Kelly decided to take a hot shower and then make a sandwich and coffee. They had been detained for five hours at the church while the police meticulously interviewed everyone.

Her investigation would have to resume the next day.

7

The Puzzle Box

Try as she might, Kelly kept coming up against a brick wall as far as the ancient text was concerned. At best, it seemed to have been written in an ancient form of Navarro-Aragonese, a completely obscure dialect that had long since fallen out of use in Spain and parts of France.

The puzzle box itself appeared to have been crafted in the early 1700s by an unknown craftsman to the royal family. According to the legend, he had crafted twelve such puzzle boxes for the young Princess Catherine. However, he seemed to have had a second, more shady set of clientele as well. It is not certain who exactly had commissioned the jeweller and clockmaker to produce that particular puzzle box, but Nicolas Fatio de Duillier, a Swiss mathematician, had been dabbling in the art of constructing these puzzle boxes for the pleasure of the royal court for almost half a century. Somehow, one of the twelve boxes, rumoured to have fallen into the wrong hands, had made its way into Aunt Judy's collection. But none of these bits of information brought her anywhere closer to finding out the truth about what the thugs were after.

In her desperation, Kelly had taken to visiting residents, particularly in the older parts of town. She attempted to converse with them in her broken, half-English, half-Spanish dialect. To the locals, she sounded like a blathering toddler, and some of them did not neglect to let her know as much. Nevertheless, she did manage to gain a sliver of information for her troubles.

Described as a romance language, Navarro-Aragonese was once spoken extensively along the Ebro River basin in the south of the Pyrenees, covering the regions of Aragon, Navarre, and La Rioja. And was seemingly spoken in a multilingual melting pot with Occitan and Basque, with the latter being the native language. This was obviously great for a scholarly treatise on Spanish languages, but it did nothing to move Kelly's investigation along. So, after days of digging, she was back to square one.

"How's my favourite sister doing?" asked Lenny cheerfully.

"I am alright, I guess," replied Kelly, trying to put on a brave front for her brother. "When are you and Laura going to pay me a visit?" she asked, trying not to show how desperately she needed him.

"About that. Kels, it is why I called. We want to come over to Lubrín for the Bread Festival in a few days from now." He stopped, as he was interrupted by Kelly's screams of delight.

"Yeah. I thought we could attend the festival, catch a cycle tour I saw scheduled for the day after, and you know, just chill with my little sister. Maybe help you out with some of the estate business or whatever. What do you think?" asked Lenny delicately – not wanting to step on Kelly's toes.

"That would be great, Len! I can't wait for you to get here. I've got so much to tell you!"

"Great. See you in a few days then. We should be there on the 19th of January," he reassured her. And with that, he rang off.

Kelly realised that Lenny and Laura would arrive in a mere two days. She whooped her way through the rest of the afternoon. Even

Esteban, a local man 'in the know' who introduced potential vendors to the business and who was particularly grumpy today, did nothing to diminish her mood. She was going to see her brother for the first time in at least six months.

Back at the flat, Kelly set to work planning an exciting itinerary for Lenny and Laura, including the Bread Festival and a local cycling competition. She would show them around the village, then take them down to Mojácar, and they would picnic in the surrounding countryside. Of course, a day trip to Granada was mandatory. It was going to be an unforgettable trip. Kelly fell asleep at her desk in the corner that served as her home office.

At around midnight, however, Kelly awoke to a distinct scraping sound outside her flat. Moonlight streamed into the lounge window and Kelly could make out the shadow of shod feet outside her door. An envelope was passed underneath. Kelly sprang into action. Racing toward the door, she yanked it open and hurtled into the hallway. But the midnight postman had disappeared.

Kelly had the presence of mind to don a pair of latex gloves. Aunt Judy always kept a box of them in the First Aid kit in the kitchen. The letter was addressed to Kelly Simpson in an old-fashioned type-written font. Carefully, she prised the envelope open so as to keep it as intact as possible. It read:

Keep your nose out of the stolen artefacts investigation. If you don't, you will not like the consequences.

"Wow. A note written in perfect English. Yet I can't seem to be able to get anyone to speak English around here. How curious!" scoffed Kelly irritably and more than a little shaken.

She called Andie immediately. Andie, in turn, contacted Inspector Gamero. Yet again, the police were at Kelly's door in the middle of the night. This is starting to become a pattern, she mused self-consciously as the neighbours came out to see what the commotion was about this time. They seemed rather put out by the constant disruptions to their sleeping patterns. This latest incident was not going to do anything for her reputation.

The policia questioned the neighbours in the hopes of getting a description of the intruder. But, as usual, nobody had seen anything. Gamero had the note and envelope dusted for prints and the whole thing was taken in as evidence; not before Kelly had taken a few pictures of the note and envelope with her mobile phone. She added it to her own stack of evidence in her personal ongoing investigation. Clearly, the local police had their own way of doing things, and she was not going to leave it to them entirely.

If anything, the note proved their top suspicion that the stolen artefacts were the work of a syndicate operating in the greater Lubrín area and not just one fly-by-night delincuente or desperado.

In the absence of any further evidence or clues, however, the mysterious warning note was thrown into the stack of evidence in the ongoing wider investigation and was soon all but forgotten.

Kelly was also pleasantly distracted by the hype of the Bread Festival and the imminent arrival of her visitors. So the investigation, and all the phantoms it tended to stir up, was placed on the back burner – at least for a few days.

Kelly made all the bookings and arrangements and allowed herself to be distracted by her need to plan everything meticulously. She even booked a bike tour of Almería, followed by an amazing and romantic day spa at an elite hotel spa nearby. One of the highlights of the spa was a huge salt pool. Customers just float on the surface of the water, relaxing and listening to the most tranquil sounds of nature. It boasted an array of pool types, offering various health-revitalising aqua therapies she knew Laura would absolutely love.

Kelly harboured a secret fear that her brother was neglecting his wife – quite unintentionally, of course. But he tended to get swept up in his work and cycling to the exclusion of everyone around him. Kelly knew that firsthand. So this time, they were visiting in her territory, and she was determined to reset the balance between Lenny's interests and Laura's – with a smattering of brother-sister bonding time thrown in for good measure, she hoped.

In the midst of all the preparations, an amusing yet viable notion struck Kelly. What if the note was planted by Andie herself? To scare me into laying off the case. I wouldn't put it past Andie to do something like that. She feels guilty for not protecting me enough. I think she promised Aunt Judy she would keep an eye on me. I guess Andie got more than she bargained for with me and all these mysterious thefts and burglaries, though.

Kelly looked into the possibility of engaging the services of a scholar on all things Spanish. Like a history professor or linguistics professor – perhaps even an archaeologist or anthropologist. She made a mental note to visit the University of Almería in the La Cañada de San Urbano district of Almería City.

The nagging feeling that she was being watched crept over Kelly, and she could not shake the feeling despite how paranoid it sounded, even in her own mind. Why would anyone want to waste their time following her around and watching her every move? She was a nobody. But Aunt Judy seemed to have been a key figure in the lives of many locals. At the same time, there seemed to be an equal number of people who seemed to have not liked her much. But Kelly could not be certain of that, as she was not yet proficient enough to understand such nuances in the language.

Kelly decided that she needed to clear her head, so she skipped off to her favourite gelato shop. Señor Gonzalo, who owned the shop, was a jolly, rotund man who sported a thick, well-kept moustache. It was his pride and joy, along with his lovely daughter, Millie, who thankfully understood a smidge of English. Enough to help her father deal with the tourists and, of course, Kelly Simpson – the estate agent whose Spanish was nowhere near fluent enough to hold a decent conversation.

"Hola, Millie, Señor Gonzalo. I'd like a choc mint gelato today, please," said Kelly, deliberately taking care to pronounce each word slowly so that Millie and her father could learn how to say the words. She also pointed out the flavour through the glass pane of the counter.

"Millie, can you read these words?" asked Kelly, hopefully. But Millie, who was very beautiful, bore a somewhat fatuous look on her face that told Kelly that she was wasting her time.

Nevertheless, Kelly spent a delightful afternoon with the Gonzalos playing sapo, a traditional game that roughly translated to Choke the Toad. It was a coin-toss game played on a large board with holes and an open-mouthed toad at the centre. The goal is to choke the frog by filling its mouth with as many coins as possible. Each player gets ten coins and has to toss the coins from a distance of about five paces away. Points are awarded for getting the coins into the frog's mouth or the holes closest to it. Some of the local children joined them in the game, and it was the distraction she needed to take her mind off things for a while. She could always count on Millie and her father to brighten her day.

A familiar face looked at her as she was leaving the gelato shop. He tossed his cigarette and walked away rapidly when Kelly caught him watching her. She tried to give chase, but he was long gone. Kelly felt a sudden chill despite the warmth of the afternoon, and she made her way swiftly to the sanctuary of her flat.

8

The Bread of Life

Kelly waited impatiently at the Almería Airport terminal – the customary box of freshly made churros in her hands. It had become one of their many rituals over the years. Lenny would prepare his brand of chilli made from scratch to welcome Kelly from one of her trips, and she would welcome him back with churros when it was his turn.

Lately, or at least since Lenny got married about five years ago, many of their traditions had fallen away, and it had left Kelly feeling somewhat cast adrift for a while. But losing Aunt Judy jarred her back to reality. She realised that she would have to put more effort into her human relationships.

Perhaps, if I had been more invested in my romance with Will, I would have picked up on the signs that he was married. Well, that is in the past, and it is high time I focused on the people in my life right now. God knows I could do with one of Lenny's big bear hugs right about now.

"There she is! Well aren't you a sight for sore eyes, li'l sis?" bellowed Lenny in his usual garrulous manner that always drew more attention than Kelly would have liked.

"Come here, you!" Lenny enveloped Kelly in his big brother arms, and she wept in relief and a shared mourning over their departed aunt who had been more of a mother and friend to them.

"Hi, Laura. Sorry for blathering on like this. How are you?" greeted Kelly, drying her eyes and giving her sister-in-law a warm hug.

"I am good thanks, Kels. How're you holding up? Lenny tells me you've had lots to deal with out here?" asked Laura, always concerned about the well-being of others.

How is it possible that someone who was born with a silver spoon in her mouth could be so selfless? Len definitely hit the jackpot when he met Laura, that's for sure, thought Kelly gratefully.

Since Aunt Judy's flat was tiny, Lenny and Laura decided to stay at the penthouse of one of Almería's finest apartment hotels, *Castillo de la Contessa*. Kelly was relieved about that because Laura was very high-maintenance despite her wonderful disposition, and Kelly was used to a much simpler lifestyle.

"I was worried about not being able to find you a suitable place in Lubrín, seeing as how it is the eve of the Bread Festival. But this penthouse suite here in Almería, is gorgeous and well worth the hour's commute into Lubrín," commented Kelly as she helped the lovebirds settle into their sprawling pad on the top floor. They even had their own private lift. The rooftop pool was heated with an adjacent jacuzzi.

"I think you two will be just fine here. Wow!" She was completely taken aback at how modern and luxurious the suite was.

"You're welcome to stay here with us, Kels. It would be awesome to catch up. We'll see how many games I can whip your butt at and then we'll binge-watch our favourite cartoons and movies from childhood. We can take you biking – come on, what do you say?" invited Lenny.

"That is a marvellous idea, honey. Kelly, it would give us a chance to catch up on our girl talk, and I can complain about your brother, and we can do girly things like mani-pedis and all that good stuff. It could be a blast. How about it?" added Laura convincingly.

"Thanks for the invitation, you guys, but you've just arrived. I'll give you some time to settle in. Meanwhile, I should try to work through the mountain of paperwork awaiting me at home. It is all very boring, I assure you. But I hope to see you both at the Bread Festival tomorrow. Don't forget that we're meeting outside the flat at ten," she reminded them on her way out.

"Welcome to the *Fiesta del Pan*!" shrieked Camilla as the thronging crowd continued to swell exponentially.

"Oh, you must be Lenny and Laura. I've seen your picture on your aunt's wall. I'm Camilla, and this is Andie."

"Pleasure to meet you both. Have you seen my sister, Camilla?" asked Lenny, his arm draped protectively over Laura's shoulders.

"She went up to the balcony. The crowd is not her shot of tequila, if you know what I mean. Shall we go up and join her?" suggested Camilla, looking at Laura's uncomfortable face.

"Sounds good. Please lead the way," concurred Lenny. So they all marched upstairs to Kelly's tiny flat.

"I'm sorry for ruining the party, you guys. I just can't handle such a huge crowd!" explained Kelly apologetically.

"Nah. We were feeling a bit claustrophobic ourselves, weren't we, hon?" replied Lenny, relieved to be out of the melee of bread and bodies.

"Ooh! Look, the procession has started. There is Saint Sebastian come out to greet everyone!" cheered Camilla appreciatively. The Bread Festival was one of her favourite times of the year.

It must be strange for Camilla to be spending the day with us instead of one of her hot young lovers, thought Kelly amusedly.

"I asked my boyfriend, Ronaldo, to collect exactly twelve bread rings for me," announced Camilla, as if reading Kelly's thoughts. "One for each month of the year! It is believed that they will bring good luck all year round."

"Does anyone know when this festival started and why?" asked Laura, curiously.

"Nobody knows, exactly. But it certainly is a lot of fun. Not to mention the fact that it keeps getting bigger and bigger each year because of the tourists the festival brings in. It has injected a much-needed financial boost to the economy, I can tell you that!" admitted Andie.

The friends watched the parade pass by and cheered wholeheartedly, participating fully in the festivities. Residents threw money and sweets at the figure of Saint Sebastian as he passed through the crowded street, and everyone seemed to be having fun.

Kelly disappeared into the kitchen to put a paella she'd ordered in advance into the oven to heat up. And she hauled out her stash of wine and tequila. Despite the limited space at the flat, Kelly and her guests had a wonderful time, and everyone enjoyed a siesta after a heavy lunch washed down with wine. By evening, the group was ready to party, so they headed out to Almería to enjoy a bit of the night scene at the local nightclubs and bars. Ronaldo joined Camilla and the rest of the party at the club.

Kelly, who did not do so well in noisy and crowded spaces, was relieved when she noticed that the club spilled over onto an open-air deck with covered spaces and lounges for groups of guests. The decor was a cosmopolitan blend of Spanish, Greek, and Moroccan influences, but the music was ultramodern, as was the menu.

It was wonderful to be surrounded by loved ones, old and new, in an exotic, exciting, faraway destination. Kelly felt safe enough to let her hair down a bit. She was taking a bit of a breather from letting Camilla and Ronaldo drag her onto the dance floor. The view of the city all lit up at night against the silhouette of the mountains in the distance made a fetching picture indeed.

"I like places like these," began a husky male voice, a bit too close to Kelly's ear for her comfort.

"I'm sorry? You must have me confused with someone else," she replied, sliding away to a more comfortable distance.

"Forgive me for intruding on your thoughts and space, Señora. I looked at you standing here enjoying the cool night air, away from the crowd, and I thought: Ah! This señora understands the importance of taking a moment to appreciate *silencio*. She is a woman after my own heart," he explained. His eyes gleamed in the darkness like a pair of luminous jewels.

"You speak English very well. Are you from around here, Señor?" asked Kelly, more to be polite than out of any genuine interest.

"I am Mateo Hernández, at your service. I do some travelling, and I am also a fan of American movies. So, perhaps my English is better than most of the locals around here. But thank you, Señora. Would you be so kind as to tell me your name?"

He seemed rather sophisticated yet grounded – a man who appreciated the finer things in life but was no stranger to a life of struggle. Probably a successful businessman who came from humble beginnings. He felt safe, but Kelly did not trust her own judgment, considering her two-year relationship fiasco with Will.

"My name is Kelly. I'm pleased to meet you, Señor Hernández," she replied politely, without encouraging familiarity.

"Please, call me Mateo. I see that you are English? What brings you to our beautiful country, Señora Kelly?" he asked, equally politely.

"I am just tying up some loose ends for a deceased relative who lived out here," she replied, trying to sound as vague as possible without fibbing – she knew she was awful at lying, so she wouldn't even hazard a try.

"Is it your work that lets you travel, Señ—I mean, Mateo?" she corrected herself, catching his warning look. Even in the dim light, Kelly could tell that his eyes were a light amber colour.

"*Sí,* it does. I deal in – antiquities. I think that is the right word," he supplied, searching for the correct word. "It is the family business, but I do have a great *pasiòn* for it too."

At once, Kelly's guard was up. Could this smooth-talking, handsome Mateo Hernández be involved in the artefact robberies?

"What do you think about the recent robberies around Lubrín?" asked Kelly, looking at him intently.

"I just got back to *Espāna* two days ago for the festival. I have been helping my uncle wind up his grandfather's considerable estate and antique collection over in the Dominican Republic for the past few months. My sister, Carmen, looks after the business here. She tells me that the *policía* come knocking on our door every time one of the robberies happens. She is very tired of answering all the same questions over and over. Now, she says, it is my turn. So I hope these bad guys get caught soon." He groaned at the prospect of being tormented by the police over the crime wave.

"Mateo, I might have a few questions for you too, but they are not about the robberies. Where are you based?" asked Kelly, intrigued by this strange, attractive man.

"Mateo!" shrieked Camilla as she jogged up to him in her spike heels, planting a kiss on each cheek.

"Camilla! *Te ves hermosa!*" replied Mateo, grinning appreciatively at Camilla's seductive tangerine-coloured cocktail dress that accentuated her every curve. The off-the-shoulder ruffled details on the sleeves drew attention to her delicate collarbones and slight shoulders. Her perfect poise gave her a statuesque silhouette.

Kelly was incredibly relieved that Camilla knew Mateo. He immediately seemed like less of a grifter to her.

"When did you get back to Almería?" asked Camilla with a pout.

"*Lo siento.* I only got back two days ago. I have not yet had a chance to even unpack my bags," he answered, chuckling.

"Mateo? Is that really you?" bellowed Lenny. "Well, isn't this a small world? Laura, look, it's Mateo Hernández from the flight!"

"Oh. *Buenas noches*, Mateo. I see you've met our Kelly," greeted Laura, her face still flushed from the liquor and dancing.

"Oh, this is your sister?" asked Mateo in genuine surprise. They chatted amiably for a while, but after a reasonable amount of chitchat, Mateo decided to take his leave.

"It was wonderful bumping into you all. We must get together before you leave *Espāna*. But I brought guests of my own, and I have been neglecting them for much too long. It was wonderful to meet you, Kelly. I hope to see you all soon. *Adiós.*" And with that, he melted into the crowd.

Kelly realised that there were other avenues to pursue in her investigation of the artefacts mystery. She made a mental note to visit Mateo's antique store in Almería soon.

There was just something liberating about cycling along an open country road with the wind in your face and the crisp, fresh air rejuvenating every cell in your body. Lenny Simpson loved everything about his life. He especially loved that his work suited his character perfectly.

As he sped along the designated route in the inter-village cycle tour, with the race starting and ending in Lubrín, he used the time to mull over a few things that had been niggling at the back of his mind lately.

Not the least of which were his neglectful ways. After Camilla had dragged Laura off onto the dance floor, Kelly, in her usual insightful manner, pointed out the fact that Laura had centred her entire life around his needs. "I mean, think about it, Len. Laura tries her best to let her plans coincide with your travel schedule so that you can be together as much as possible, right?"

"Yeah. She is an angel, Kel. I've got no complaints. And even when she can't travel with me because of her charity work commitments, she makes damn sure that everything is perfect for me when I get back. I don't know how she does it all, Kel, honestly," extolled Lenny unabashedly.

"I am so glad that you can acknowledge all the meticulous little ways that Laura shows you how much she loves you, bro. But do you ever plan a trip with her interests in mind?"

"How do you mean?"

"Well, you know how Laura is always trying to make life easier for the less fortunate, right? So, have you ever considered maybe doing some volunteer work together in a place that is ravaged by famine or something? Or taking her to a place that she has always wanted to experience that does not involve extreme sports or cycling?"

"Come to think of it, she did mention how much she would love to put a team together to educate young women in the Middle East or Africa, where there is little focus on education for girls. I support the idea, but I guess I never really gave her the kind of active support she might be looking for. Sis! You are a genius! Thank you," he gushed as the lightbulb moment took effect.

"I am glad to help. I really like Laura, and I think she deserves the best my bro can offer her. I have some surprises for the two of you while you're here, too. After your cycling tour, I will be taking full command of your itinerary! That's an order!" she warned in her most convincing mock army general voice.

"Ma'am! Yes, Ma'am!" he mocked right back, saluting.

I really need to up my game with my lady, that's for sure. Our marriage must be an equal partnership. Especially after hearing that we can't have kids, she seems so much more vulnerable. Time to step up, Lenny, my boy.

The local royal and celebrity around Almería, the Duque Carlos Miguel Luis XI, handed Lenny his third-place rosette. "Congratulations, Mr Simpson. I see that cycling talent runs in the family. Your aunt was also an avid cyclist. Too bad about her accident. My condolences to you and your family," offered the coldly sophisticated Duque in his stiff upper-lipped manner. There was just something about the way he said it that made the hairs at the back of Lenny's neck prickle.

"Thank you, Your Grace. You knew my aunt?" asked Lenny in bewilderment.

"I make it my business to know everyone in my town, Mr Simpson – even the foreigners who have come to call Lubrín their home," explained the Duque with mock patience.

After that strange encounter with the decidedly creepy Duque, Lenny thought he'd hit the shower at the cycling club before meeting Laura for lunch at the Tapas Lounge. He took his leave of the Duque and went into the locker room.

Lenny was the last to get into the shower, and the place was quite deserted by the time he was done. A cloud of steam enveloped the whole place, and it reminded him of their visit to Niagara Falls some years back. Just then, Lenny heard a shuffle of footsteps.

"Hola? Is anyone there?" he asked cautiously.

Without warning, a knobbly hand grabbed Lenny's forearm. A short, ancient-looking old man, who was badly hunched, spoke to him in Spanish. *"Tu tìa fue asesinada!"* The strange man repeated these words over and over as he slipped away through the steamed-up room. Lenny dressed as fast as he could and ran outside to try to catch up with the old man, but he was nowhere to be found. Even though his Spanish was somewhat rusty, one word from what the old man had said stuck in his mind – '*asesinada*' meant 'murdered.' *He was trying to tell me that Aunt Judy was murdered. I am sure of it. I can't tell Kelly what happened here. It will freak her out even more. I need to get to the bottom of Aunt Judy's death on my own,* he resolved pensively.

But all too soon, it was time to leave Spain and return to the office in London.

9

Making Contacts

Kelly was lost in a daydream about the whirlwind holiday visit by Lenny and Laura. Somehow, the week they'd spent together had felt like mere hours – cherished moments she would keep in her heart forever. She replayed their adventures on repeat in her mind. They were a great source of comfort and strength to her in the empty days that followed.

Lenny had asked her to find out everything she could about the Lubrín Cycling Club and the people who ran it. He especially wanted her to look up information about the Duque Carlos Miguel Luis XI. The Duque had given Lenny a creepy vibe. Even though he claimed to have known Aunt Judy well, there was just something about his smug sneer that set off alarm bells in Lenny's mind.

Lenny had not told Kelly about his encounter with the old man. He thought she had enough to deal with as it was, without him adding to her stress with the babbling ramblings of an old, decrepit man he'd met in the men's locker room. But he did beg her to leave Spain and come back to England with them. His words rang in her mind.

"Kels, I wish you'd reconsider staying here. The culture is pleasant enough, and I am glad you're making friends. But this whole stolen artefacts business has got me on edge. I would much rather have you back on English soil, where I can count on the Alfriston coppers to keep you safe. East Sussex is so much safer than Lubrín, Almería, li'l sis. What do you say?" implored Lenny with his puppy dog green eyes with their scattering of golden flecks that lit up when he laughed.

Kelly thought back to her tiny English village. Some of the ancient architecture dated back to the fourteenth century, like St. Andrew's Church. She did miss walking along the scenic Cuckmere River, especially in the summer months. Her flat, which Judy had helped her buy for a song, held wonderful memories of a happier time. But Kelly felt that too much had happened, and she had somehow been changed by recent events.

I wonder how Lenny would feel if he found out that I've been toying with the idea of moving to Spain permanently. But I will only tell him once I've made my decision for certain, mused Kelly, worried about what her brother would say.

The sound of her office phone ringing from what seemed like miles away finally interrupted her reverie. "Hola, Hello. Fargo Estate Agents, this is Kelly Simpson speaking. How may I help you?" I have got to learn to say this in Spanish someday, she thought, not for the first time.

"Hola, Señora Simpson. I am Isabella Ruiz. I was sorry to hear about the passing of my dear friend, Señora Fargo," came the lilting voice of the woman on the other end of the line. Her thick Spanish accent further enhanced the musicality of her voice.

"Gracias, Señora Ruiz, is it?" asked Kelly, faltering as she was only just coming out of her daydream.

"Sí, Señora Simpson. I was wondering if we could chat over afternoon tea?"

"Er... thank you for the invitation, Señora Ruiz. But would you mind telling me what this is all about?" asked Kelly, cautiously. She would not give Lenny a chance to say, 'I told you so.'

"Of course. I am the head of the Spanish Heritage and Preservation Society here in Almería. I believe your aunt's extensive collection of Spanish artefacts has now fallen into your care, is that not so?" she asked. It was a mere formality – this woman had clearly done her homework before calling.

"Sí. That is correct, Señora. But I have to inform you that I have been appointed the sole custodian of the collection, and I intend to keep it intact for as long as possible," replied Kelly frankly.

"Why don't you visit us at the Almería museum one afternoon and let me show you why we would love to display your aunt's collection amongst our impressive array of artefacts?" Isabella suggested, with a hint of impatience bubbling under the surface of her sophisticated, polished manners.

"I will definitely think about taking you up on that offer one day," replied Kelly, evasively. "Unfortunately, I am swamped with work and my schedule is pretty tight at present. But I will call you to schedule a meeting over tea soon. Thank you for calling, but I really must get back to work now. Sorry I couldn't be more helpful, Señora. Hasta la vista."

Kelly, who was usually incredibly polite, was starting to find Camilla's coaching rather useful in dealing with pushy people like Señora Ruiz. She felt a sense of achievement after worming her way out of a tea date with the old historian. Even though Kelly did need lots of help working out the details of why the artefacts were suddenly so fiercely sought after – to the extent that people would kill to have them – she knew that Isabella Ruiz had less than honourable intentions toward Aunt Judy's collection.

In fact, Kelly had started making a list of people to look into and, without hesitation, added Isabella Ruiz to the list which also included the Duque whatshisname and Mateo Hernández, even though he was friendly with her people, she still wanted to check out his background. She found it more than a little suspicious that he had tried to befriend her and then backed off once he realised she was with Lenny and the crew.

Kelly decided that it was high time she tracked down a specialist in the field of all things Spanish, so she contacted the Department of History at the University of Almería. The head of the department was conducting a field trip to Vélez-Blanco Castle. The trip had only just commenced and Kelly thought she would be able to meet up with the professor at the castle.

Fortunately, she made it to Vélez-Blanco just as the students were disembarking the rickety old bus that had miraculously delivered them safely. Joining the tour as if she were a student, Kelly caught a glimpse of Professor Dimitri Vázquez. He was quite attractive in a studious, bookwormish sort of way – just the kind that Kelly found appealing. His luminous brown eyes, shaded by the longest eyelashes Kelly had seen on a man, gave him an appearance of innocence that was, thankfully, rescued by the firm set to his jawline. A rather aristocratic nose tapered down to his full lips, which Kelly found quite hypnotic as he spoke rapidly in Spanish.

All Kelly knew about the place was that the castle was built by the Governor of Murcia, Marquis Pedro Fajardo, who was the first Marquis of Los Vélez. According to legend, the castle had been built on the ruins of an ancient Islamic fortress. The Marquis wished to preside over the town from the vantage point of his castle, asserting his dominance over Los Vélez.

Kelly found it rather difficult to concentrate on her surroundings as she found herself quite mesmerised by the professor in his cliché lecturer attire: patched-elbow sports jacket; snug, and rather flattering, pair of blue jeans; and leather boots. A cross-body bag slung across his chest over a simple white shirt with blue and gold lines running down it gave him a nerdy-chic appearance. Kelly pegged his age to be around thirty-five, but his full head of jet-black hair, worn brushed back with a centre part, gave him a deceptively youthful appearance. So Kelly was uncertain about how old the professor actually was.

After the formal tour, students were free to explore the castle and its surrounds, stopping to do a quick sketch or take a few photographs. Several students broke off into groups and were already setting up picnic spots on the grounds and under the trees. Kelly found the view utterly breathtaking and snapped off a good number of pictures herself before heading off to find the professor for a one-on-one chat.

She was hoping that he spoke English fluently. She caught sight of her reflection in a large mirror in the foyer and realised that she looked a mess. Reaching into her bag, she pulled out a travel hairbrush she usually hardly bothered with and gave her unruly hair a quick brush through. She also touched up her lip colour and spritzed a bit of perfume that Camilla insisted a woman should always keep in her bag. Feeling fresh and moderately presentable, Kelly went off in search of the professor.

He was standing beneath a huge arch explaining away to a group of young students who were obviously smitten by him. The professor was completely unaware of their admiring glances as he spoke animatedly about the architecture. Kelly found his energy and enthusiasm quite attractive, and he looked rather fetching inside the ornate environment of the castle's interior. Taking a deep breath to fortify herself, Kelly approached the group. She stood directly in the professor's field of vision and immediately caught his eye. In fact, as their eyes met, he lost his place in the explanation and abruptly fell silent.

The group of young ladies giggled at his befuddlement at the sight of Kelly, and they left Dimitri Vázquez floundering in the presence of Kelly Simpson, the equally awkward and bookish visitor.

"Hola. Are you Professor Dimitri Vázquez?" she asked timidly.

"Sí, I am. And you are...?" he asked in perfect English. Kelly breathed a sigh of relief.

"Thank goodness you can speak English. My name is Kelly Simpson. I was hoping I could pick your brain for a bit, Professor," admitted Kelly immediately.

"Oh? Do you have an interest in Spanish history, Señora Simpson?" He brushed his hand through his hair – the only sign of his nervousness at being in such close proximity to Kelly.

"As a matter of fact, I am incredibly fascinated by Spanish history, and I was hoping you could help me solve a few pieces of a puzzle I have been trying to figure out. Is that okay?" she asked hopefully.

"Unfortunately, Señora Simpson, I have little time for treasure hunts and such business. My interests are purely academic, and I am very busy—"

"Oh, no. You've misunderstood me. I, I need some help tracing some artefacts I have recently inherited from my aunt, who spent a large part of her life here. It would seem as though some very dangerous people wish to get their hands on them, and I would like to discover why that is. Would you be so kind as to help me? I assure you that you will in no way be placed in harm's way," she rambled.

"It sounds like this is a matter best left to the policía to resolve..." he began.

"Oh, no. The police have their hands full with all the other related crimes. I am sure you have heard about all the petty thefts that have been taking place in Lubrín and the surrounding villages, Professor?"

"Sí, I have indeed. Is that why you feel that the artefacts you've inherited are in danger?" he asked, trying to connect the dots.

"Something like that. But I also want to know more about their origins and who may have commissioned them. I also found a message inscribed on one of the artefacts and I would like some help translating the words as they are in a language that is no longer in use..." She trailed off as she realised that she must sound like quite a loon to the handsome professor.

"I am not sure how much help I can be to you, Señora Simpson—"

"Please, call me Kelly," she interrupted, beaming. "When can we meet?"

"Er... How about Friday afternoon at three? Here is my card with the details about my office. See you there, Señora Simp—I mean, Kelly," he suggested.

"Friday afternoon it is then. Thank you, Professor," she confirmed.

"De nada. Hasta la próxima vez, Kelly Simpson," he called cheerily as he walked toward another group that needed his attention.

10

Dredging Up the Past

"So, you think your aunt may have somehow become involved with those thugs who have been stealing artefacts from the old families in Almería?" asked Dimitri Vázquez incredulously.

"You know, Dimitri, I even suspect that it's what ultimately got her killed."

"You don't think it was an accident?" Kelly knew the question was rhetorical, so just shrugged. "Alright, let's get to work. Tell me everything you can about these artefacts. Do you have pictures of them?" Dimitri rolled up his sleeves while logging into his laptop.

Kelly filled him in on everything she thought might be useful to their investigation.

"I would love to know what those curious symbols on every piece mean, and I am hoping that you can help me translate the inscription I found inside the puzzle box. These seem like good places to start, don't you think?"

"*Sí*, I am glad you came to me with this. I think it will help me direct my new study focus," replied Dimitri. They were both happy to have met, and it was a treat to be working together.

"I have a great idea. Why don't I take you to Aunt Judy's country villa, and you can examine the collection for yourself?" Kelly's smile showed her excitement.

"Are you sure?" asked the bashful professor.

"Of course! We can make a day of it. I will take care of everything but I suggest you bring a camera too. I know it's really ambitious of me, but perhaps we can document each piece and try to trace its origin?" asked Kelly, the hope clear in her voice.

"That sounds like fun. I will be busy with lectures and grading papers for the rest of the week," admitted Dimitri, frowning as if trying to remember his schedule.

"I also have work stuff to see to. How about we make a weekend of it? If your wife or girlfriend doesn't mind you spending the weekend with another woman, that is?" joked Kelly, laughing awkwardly.

"I, I don't have... That won't be a problem," replied Dimitri. However, his laugh portrayed nervousness.

The rest of the week dragged on interminably. On the positive side of things, Kelly managed to resolve the issue of the land acquisition by the Brit who never bothered to secure the proper identification number.

"Andie, I really think we should look into these three people more closely," Kelly said emphatically. She had given Andie the list of names she'd been compiling: the Duque, the Historian, and the dealer of antiquities.

"Come now, Kelly. I can't go poking around into the lives of all those you find to be dodgy. I will need more to go on before I can legitimately start digging up dirt on random people you don't trust," retorted Andie.

Kelly had to ring off as a rather flamboyant peacock of a man strode into the office. He planted his crocodile-skinned shoes in the centre of the room and did a complete sweep of the place. *He could not have been more dramatic if he'd worn a velvet cape,* thought Kelly, stifling her laughter.

"I am Diego Reyes, and I am looking for Señora Fargo's successor," he announced to the floor in general, bowing with a flourish. *He may as well be a court jester!* thought Kelly as she took in his purple velvet suit and psychedelic pocket handkerchief. A bejewelled black cane completed his ensemble.

"*Hola*, Señor Reyes. My name is Kelly Simpson. How may I help you today?" Kelly called out, standing up so that he would make his way to her. *How I wish Camilla were here right now.* This was not the first time she had wished this today. Camilla had gone to evaluate an estate out in a remote village outside Lubrín and would only be back later that afternoon, if at all, knowing Camilla.

"I have been offering to buy Judy Fargo's country estate for a few years now. But every time she gave me the same non-committal answer: 'I will definitely consider your offer.' Well, Judy is no longer with us. God bless her soul. *In nomine Patris et Filii, et Spiritus Sancti.*" He performed the symbol of the cross over his upper body and kissed his thumb, looking up dramatically.

Oh boy! What a character!

"Thank you, Señor. But I am not ready to sell off my aunt's property yet. In fact, her properties and possessions are still in the process of being transferred into my name. It has scarcely been a month since her passing, you know?" Kelly reminded him, glowering at his arrogant and overbearing intrusion.

"Forgive me, Señora Simpson. May I call you Kelly?" he asked offhandedly.

"Señora Simpson will be fine," was the curt response. "I appreciate your offer and will take it into consideration. Now, if you will excuse me, I have a business to run. Thank you. Kindly, see yourself out." And with that, she turned her attention to her laptop. The peacock left in a huff and a puff, muttering to himself in Spanish with a few *"Santa Marías"* thrown in for good measure. He turned back to look threateningly at Kelly several times before disappearing from sight.

Kelly jotted down his name and made a note to add him to her list of "persons of interest" she had going. She would ask Camilla about him when she got back.

"Ronaldo and I want to join you two at the mansion. Come on, what do you say, Kelly darling? We will show you two how to have a good time, no?" teased Camilla – she was only half-joking and secretly hoped that Kelly would invite them to join the weekend getaway at Judy's villa. More so that she could watch over Kelly than enjoy the lovely place. The memory of what happened the last time Kelly was at the villa still sent chills through Camilla. Besides, who knew what the two of them could unearth if left unattended?

"The last thing I need is for you and your pretty boy Ronnie to corrupt the one person who may actually be able to help me get to the bottom of all these mysterious occurrences and petty theft here in Lubrín," pouted Kelly, licking her dessert spoon appreciatively.

They were enjoying their usual Friday afternoon ice cream ritual at the gelato place across the street from the office. Camilla had no choice but to capitulate – she couldn't risk Kelly growing suspicious at this crucial point in time.

"Funny thing happened while you were out today. Do you know a Diego Reyes, by any chance?" asked Kelly irritably. The mere memory of that pompous man with his loud clothes and chunky jewellery gave her the creeps.

"Oh, him. He didn't try to make an offer on Judy's villa, did he? He wouldn't – He did?" Kelly simply nodded, tucking into a generous spoonful of her cookies 'n cream flavoured ice cream.

"He has been after that estate for years! But Judy wouldn't budge, of course. She couldn't..." Camilla caught herself in the nick of time and stopped talking.

"Why? Why couldn't Aunt Judy have sold the mansion? Camilla, what aren't you telling me?" Kelly bolted upright in their tiny booth.

"I just meant that Judy had strict standards. She wouldn't sell to a shady businessman and politician like Diego Reyes, of all people. Some say that he has ties with mobsters in Madrid," whispered Camil-la.

"I swear, Kelly. You are becoming more and more paranoid by the day. I am your friend. I have no reason to lie to you, Kels. Now, let's talk about what lingerie you are going to pack for your weekend away with Professor Hotbod," she said, making her eyebrows dance mischievously while she shimmied her shoulders in glee.

Kelly threw a bunch of peanut toppings at Camilla in response.

Kelly had prepared meticulously for the weekend trip and had got an array of wines, cheeses, and easy-to-prepare meals. She also arranged for the usual staff that cleaned and maintained the place to be in attendance.

They met at Dimitri's flat in Almería early Saturday. Since his vehicle of choice was a stunning black Ducati, which Kelly refused to admit she found irresistibly attractive, they took her car. At least it had been Judy's car – a versatile black top-of-the-range Jeep.

They talked about the history of the region along the way. Kelly tried to steer the conversation toward his family, but he diverted her attention to the town they had been passing through instead, so she let it go.

Andrés Santiago, the all-round handyman, butler, and manager of the estate, welcomed them and helped with their bags. His wife, Julia, was the housekeeper and cook. When Aunt Judy would be there on holiday or for the weekend, the couple stayed on the property in the cottage by the pool. Kelly wished she could speak Spanish well so that she could learn more about this charming middle-aged couple.

After a scrumptious brunch, expertly prepared by Julia, Kelly took Dimitri for a tour around the property, finishing at the museum. "Incredible," he managed to get out as his jaw hit the floor. "Your aunt sure made it her life's work to gather this impressive collection. What will you do with it now?" he asked curiously.

"Honestly, I haven't decided yet. I suspect that these items may have belonged to an important collection once. Look, these are the symbols I was telling you about." Kelly gestured as she turned over an ornately carved wooden piece. The relief features were inlaid with gold and semi-precious jewels. It was a rather eclectic piece depicting a woman facing a panel of men.

"Curious. These look like runes or some other ancient symbols. I will have to do some research and get back to you on this. I have not come across these symbols before," admitted Dimitri, absorbed in his study of the artefacts. They spent the rest of the day taking pictures and reading up on the collections from the ancient Spanish families.

By mid-afternoon, Julia breezed in with a tea tray laden with snacks. "You eat. Rest," insisted Julia good-naturedly. She brought some wine and a cheese board with crackers into the study, where they could enjoy the warm afternoon sun.

Just then, a beautiful black cat with the most startling emerald and black eyes strolled into the study and wedged itself under the teak desk.

"*Hola*, cute kitty," cooed Kelly, following the furry black streak under the desk.

Kelly slipped into the crawl space to bring the cat up to the couch so she could stroke it and spoil it with goodies from the tea tray. "Here, kitty-kitty. *Psssst.*" She lured it into her arms. "That's right. Come to mamma, little kitty," she crooned, stroking its luxurious fur. But she bumped her head with a thud on her way out, and they both heard a loud click. "What on earth..." She had accidentally opened a secret drawer under the desk.

"Dimitri, come and take a look at..." But he was already there. They peered into the drawer together. In it was a single, well-loved book.

"Did you get hurt?" he asked sweetly. Kelly shook her head, too distracted by the discovery to pay attention to her throbbing head.

The book was written in ancient Spanish. "Well, I guess I will leave it to you to make sense of this one, Prof. But I wonder why Aunt Judy hid it away in there," she mused excitedly.

"It is all very – *¿Cómo se dice?* – mysterious?" concurred Dimitri.

"And where did you come from, you cute little furball? It was you who helped us find the secret drawer. I think you deserve a treat." Kelly allowed herself to be distracted by the cat while Dimitri retired to the furthest corner of the library to study the ancient text in peace.

Within a few minutes, Julia returned and Kelly squealed as the cook set down an amazingly colourful platter of nachos with the most delicious toppings on the sideboard. But Dimitri was completely absorbed in the text and would not let up until he had read it. Julia gave him a quizzical look and insisted that he take a break, but it seemed like he hadn't even heard her, so she left with a worried look on her face that Kelly found rather strange.

Kelly pottered around the library while Dimitri pored over the book until, out of the blue, he said, "Kelly, I think I've found something. You know that artwork on the wooden panel you showed me earlier? I saw something similar in this book."

Dimitri's determination to overcome the old dialect had paid finally paid off. "This book is about the Spanish Inquisition. There is a story of a supposed witch who had survived the Inquisition twice! This is incredible!" marvelled Dimitri. He began explaining as he read.

They learned that Paula de Eguiluz was something of a legend in her time. She was descended from an African slave woman named Guiomar in what is known as Santo Domingo today. Paula lived with her mother in the household of Diego de Leguizamòn until she was eventually sold to Íñigo de Otaza, who bought her when she was merely a teenager. After several years had passed, she was eventually sold to Juan de Eguiluz in Havana. She was later brought to Cartagena to stand trial for witchcraft and was exiled from Cuba upon her conviction. Cartagena was a port city where a rich exchange of healing methods and medical treatments took place. Unfortunately, all the intercontinental mixing also served to increase exposure to sickness and disease.

It was often up to healers such as Paula de Eguiluz to create cures for these new illnesses that plagued the people of the city. However, the Spaniards and Creoles viewed the healer women with suspicion –

accusing them of bringing about the illnesses in the first place. As a result of her success as a healer, Paula had been accused of witchcraft on three separate occasions between 1623 and 1636.

The first trial took place in 1624 and the allegations against Paula shook the entire community. Her Cuban neighbours alleged that Paula had killed her owner's newborn baby by sucking on its navel. She had survived a fall unscathed after jumping out of a window to evade her master's whip. She had been accused of practising dark erotic magic and of making a pact with the devil. It was also believed that she would hold secret gatherings of her coven of witches, where they would hatch unspeakable plans to wreak havoc among the good people of Cartagena. Paula explained away the allegations and asserted that her accusers were envious of her master's affections for her and her extensive and trendy wardrobe of clothing – much too extravagant for a slave woman.

This trial dragged on for a period of three months, during which time, she had been subjected to thirteen hearings. Eventually, Paula realised that the only way to be rid of these hearings was to admit to being a witch, even though she did not practice witchcraft. So she told them what they wanted to hear even though it was a lie, and her punishment was said to be about 200 lashes in public, and she had to serve two years in the general hospital. She had to wear the sambenito – a scapulary worn by the repentant found guilty by the Spanish Inquisition.

However, her peace was short-lived, for, in 1632, Paula was arrested for the second time under the suspicion that she had returned to the practice of witchcraft and had renewed her pact with the devil. It was true that Paula used her freedom to associate with other women who dabbled in love potions and enchantments that were believed to have sway over the minds of male patrons. Paula worked as a washerwoman and healer and had several raging love affairs. This trial resulted in twenty-one hearings, during which Paula knew what the Inquisitors wanted to hear. She admitted to practising healing and witchcraft in her efforts to help and heal people – especially with their sexual problems. She also named twenty-one women who were also witches and devil worshippers, just so she could walk free.

A third trial came about in order to revisit the evidence presented in the second one. At least five women among the twenty-one named by Paula came forward, claiming that Paula had inducted them into devil worship. Paula faced a very real threat of being executed. She spoke exclusively of her healing work during this trial, steering clear of all links to devil worship. Her words worked, and she was allowed to live once more.

An exceedingly wealthy businessman of the New World, Bishop Pérez de Lazarraga, sought Paula's expertise in the healing arts, and they eventually had a passionate, secret love affair.

Some accounts claim that they were caught, and she was finally burned at the stake, while other accounts of her life claim that she managed to escape and fled to Spain. She had been pregnant with Lazarraga's child at the time and settled in a remote village. Some say that she had amassed an impressive collection of art and valuables from around the world, and that each piece had been infused with her magic and witchcraft.

They also read about a prophecy associated with Paula de Eguiluz's descendants. But this prophecy is only known to a select few who have pledged their lives to keeping it a secret from others who, in turn, have pledged their lives to ensuring the prophecy will never be fulfilled.

"But what is the prophecy? I bet she settled somewhere in Almería!" Kelly was bursting with excitement at this development.

"She was a healer and an opportunist in equal measure. Her legacy must have lived on in her child. I am certain that the prophecy has to do with her lineage," added Dimitri, equally enthralled.

"But what does all of this have to do with Aunt Judy's collection?"

"Do you think that these artefacts are from Paula de Eguiluz's collection? If so, why would anyone be so determined to get their hands on it if she was, in fact, a witch?" reasoned Dimitri.

Meanwhile, from the safety of the pool house, Andrés reported in Spanish, "They are onto the truth." He then hung up and continued with his chores.

Kelly and Dimitri spent the evening poring over other books in Judy's library, trying to find any information about the prophecy and the symbols imprinted on the artefacts but to no avail. They returned to Lubrín the next day, resolving to meet soon to discuss other avenues they could try. Dimitri vowed to keep their findings a secret, as it was clear that they had somehow stumbled upon the reasons the residents of Andalucia were embroiled in an ancient battle between opposing factions.

How many people were involved and what Aunt Judy had to do with any of it remained to be seen. Kelly wondered how much Camilla and Andie knew about Paula and her legacy. Kelly decided that she would tell them what she and Dimitri had learned and then ask them if they knew anything about it. Kelly hated secrets and lies, especially from those she trusted.

11

Sleuthing Solo

Kelly got back to her flat late Sunday afternoon, and she was astonished to find that the place had been broken into and ransacked. A message was scrawled across a wall in the lounge: "Curiosity killed the cat! Stop digging, little kitty!"

Andie and Camilla arrived within minutes of her calls, and the police trailed in almost an hour later.

"Kelly, are you alright?" asked Andie, who was the first to arrive. "Can you tell if they took anything?"

"Nothing, as far as I can see, Andie. But I will have to do a thorough check," replied Kelly, still shaken.

"But who would do this to you?" asked Camilla, pacing rapidly in the tiny space.

"I am starting to think that Lenny might be right. You should go back to England. You'd be safer there," suggested Andie. Kelly caught the warning look Camilla sent her and the slight shake of her head.

"Not a chance. And I will thank you to not let him hear of this, please, ladies," warned Kelly.

"Suit yourself, but I will have to assign someone on protection detail to you if you insist on investigating this case. No arguments!" warned Andie in return.

By now, the neighbours had grown quite used to these regular disturbances and the police presence at the English woman's flat at all hours of the night, and they soon lost interest, returning to their ordinary lives. Of course, nobody had seen or heard anything. There were no fingerprints to be found anywhere. The door had been jimmied open, and a locksmith had to be called out from Albox. He would only be able to attend to it the next day.

"That's it, Kelly. I want you to pack a bag and come stay with me," instructed Camilla, assuming control of the disaster.

"Oh, no, Camilla, I can't impose on you again," began Kelly. But Camilla wouldn't hear of it.

Kelly realised that it might give her a chance to confront Camilla and suss out how much she and Andie knew about the whole thing.

"Actually, that might be a good idea after all. I guess I will have to discuss what Dimitri and I learned with you both, and your place would be ideal. Andie, do you think you could join us at Camilla's?"

So the three women bunked down for a sleepover at Camilla's cosy house. They planned on going into the office as late as possible the next day.

Kelly brought over the mountain of food Julia sent back with her, and the women feasted on traditional rustic Spanish cuisine while Kelly bore a barrage of teasing about Dimitri from the older women.

But the time soon arrived for Kelly to spill the details about her findings. She told them about the mysterious cat and the secret drawer in the desk, the book, and Paula de Eguiluz.

"That is a very interesting story indeed," responded Andie, after listening intently to Kelly's recounting of events. "But what's got me completely stumped is what all of this had to do with Judy Fargo."

"I think, with a little more digging, we should be able to uncover the details about the prophecy of Paula de Eguiluz. I am betting that whatever the connection to Aunt Judy, it has to do with that prophecy," concluded Kelly, feeling more convinced the more she thought about it.

"Come on, Kelly!" burst out Camilla. "The writing is *literally* on the wall for Chrissakes! Just leave it well alone already!" She threw her hands up in exasperation and looked at Andie for support.

"I think that Camilla may be onto something here, Kelly," she offered gently. "Look, I know you want to get to the bottom of everything that's been going on – we all do. But I think that we should leave this to the local police."

And then, looking at the doubtful expression on Kelly's face, she added, "And I will also call in a few favours from my contacts in MI6." Catching the look on Camilla's face, though, Andie decided to add a further warning to her speech.

"But we are clearly dealing with criminal types who will not hesitate to kill anyone who gets in their way. It would be foolhardy to try to solve this mystery on your own," she advised.

"But I am not on my own, am I? I've got you two and Dimitri. Not to mention the completely competent local police department," Kelly added sarcastically.

Andie and Camilla exchanged meaningful looks, then a pregnant silence followed.

"You guys are scaring me. What aren't you telling me here?"

"Kelly, this isn't easy for us to tell you. And we've tried to put it off in the hopes that those goons would back off," began Camilla, sniffling into a paper towel.

"Judy wanted us to keep you out of this legacy nonsense as much as possible," added Andie.

"What do you mean by 'legacy nonsense', Andie?" asked Kelly, sitting bolt upright and looking from one to the other.

"Your mother and Aunt Judy are descendants of Paula de Eguiluz," blurted out Camilla – the strain was proving too much for her to bear.

"But – not to sound like a bigot or anything here – Paula had African ancestry – and we're as white as can be," reasoned Kelly.

"Yes, but that is because every one of your relatives since Paula has been Caucasian, but the bloodline has remained intact," explained Andie.

"So, you mean I am the great-great-whatever descendant of Paula – the witch?" asked Kelly, incredulously.

Andie and Camilla nodded simultaneously. "But what do these criminals have to do with us?" Kelly finally asked the most important question of the day.

"We were not privy to that information," Andie answered, and Camilla nodded in agreement. "However," she continued, "we do know that Judy wanted us to protect you at all costs. You are very valuable for some reason unbeknownst to us."

Kelly sat back in her chair, utterly shocked at the information she'd just heard. "But why haven't either of you bothered to mention this to me before?" Kelly's anger was mounting as she pieced together all the ways in which she had been placed in danger due to her ignorance about who she was.

"How many of the townsfolk know who I am?" asked Kelly, bracing herself for the answer.

"A few of the older people might know, I guess," answered Camilla, and waved a hand vaguely.

"That would explain why some of them look at me with such fear and distrust!" spat Kelly in disgust – the realisation finally dawned on her about the reason for the mixed reactions to her by the townsfolk.

Later, in bed, Kelly examined every inch of the secret book. Nestled inside the cover of the book, which she carefully pried open, was a thick piece of parchment that had yellowed with time. A second, more recent piece of parchment lay behind it. These two bits of paper detailed the lineage of Paula de Eguiluz right down to Lenny and herself.

But why is this lineage so important? Surely they can tell that we are just ordinary folks! thought Kelly in frustration. *Perhaps this book is what the burglar was looking for at my flat. They need confirmation that Lenny and I are her descendants.*

Kelly decided to keep the list a secret and snapped off pictures of it and the book just in case the hard copies went missing. Just to be thorough, she carefully pulled apart the back cover of the book but found nothing. Disappointed, she decided to investigate the spine for good measure. At last, her diligence was rewarded – affixed to the spine of the book was an ancient key. The handle of the key bore the same symbol of the three concentric circles that formed a sort of ripple. The key seemed to be made from some sort of gold alloy.

Hello, what do we have here? Now I wonder what secrets you are protecting, little key, mused Kelly – her sleuthing skills were at full power with this latest discovery.

She turned the key over in her hands – the gum used to secure it had also served to preserve it. Kelly decided that she would keep this key to herself. She placed it on her chain with the half-heart pendant Aunt Judy had given her all those years ago.

In the morning, Kelly went off to visit Dimitri at the university. She recounted what Camilla and Andie finally revealed to her about her heritage and even showed him the family tree. But she omitted the details about having discovered the key. Kelly decided to trust nobody until she uncovered the truth.

"It turns out that I have witch blood running in my veins, Professor. So, you'd better watch out, or I could turn you into a frog!" she joked, and they both had a hearty laugh.

"It finally makes sense why you have become a target, Kelly. I am glad you were not harmed in the burglary," he said softly. His honey-coloured eyes were full of concern.

"Actually, it really makes no sense at all. Why do you think they are after me?"

"Well – I think that perhaps they probably belong to a conservative Catholic sect that wishes to wipe out all the descendants of Paula de Eguiluz. Maybe your aunt really was murdered. Which means that you are their next target. I think you should go back to England. It is not safe for you here," urged Dimitri.

"I am not going anywhere until Aunt Judy's murderers are behind bars!" she replied vehemently, slamming her hand on his desk.

"The reason I came to see you, Dimitri, is that I need your help to uncover what the prophecy is about. Do you think you will be able to dig it up?" Kelly's expression held hope.

"I will give it a try, but it might take a while. It will be like looking for a needle in a haystack," he admitted.

"Okay, while you are working on it from here, I think I'm gonna head back to Aunt Judy's country villa. I have a hunch that there is more to discover there."

They decided to meet the next afternoon. "Kelly, please be careful. I think I should come with you," offered Dimitri, despite the mountain of work he had himself.

"No, thanks. I appreciate the offer, but I will be fine on my own."

Kelly thought it best to wait for the cover of night to go back to the villa. She knew the Santiagos were off visiting their daughter in Madrid, and they were not due to return for at least a week. It was the perfect time to do a bit of snooping without interruptions.

The villa looked rather eerie in the darkness. Only the solar-powered garden lights were on. Kelly knew that they were on a timer and would switch off automatically at dawn. It was quite effortless to deactivate the recently restored security system and enter the villa, since Andrés had shown her how it worked. Kelly was reluctant to admit it, but she found something off about the middle-aged couple. They appeared harmless enough on the surface, but Kelly just couldn't shake the feeling that they were not as well-intentioned as they seemed. *Or it could just be my super-paranoid imagination running away with me!* she chided herself as she made her way to the study.

This was where we discovered the hidden drawer. Perhaps the cabinet that this key unlocks might also be somewhere in here.

Unfortunately, after an intensive two-hour search, Kelly had to admit that she had been mistaken. There was nothing more to find in the study. But she refused to give up. Her gut feeling told her that the lock matching the key around her neck was somewhere on the property, and she was determined to find it. She would start in the oldest section of the house – the master bedroom. According to Andrés, the original villa had been much smaller and simpler. It was only in the early 1970s that the place received a complete facelift, with the other wings added on to increase the resale value of the property. It was Kelly's grandparents – whom she had never met – who had seen to the renovations. And, when Kelly's mum passed away, Judy became its custodian. Now the place belonged to Kelly.

Feeling like an interloper on her own property, Kelly had never ventured into the master bedroom during her previous stay. Besides, the study had held more fascination for her. Stepping into the bedroom now, she felt like she was in the midst of the film set of a Spanish soap opera. The colour scheme of the place was an off-white and tangerine palette with a smattering of azure in places. An impressive array of what looked like original oil canvases decorated the room. One painting in particular struck Kelly as especially masterful. It was the only painting on the stone feature wall.

The painting depicted a dark-skinned woman with long, wild hair. She wore a white dress with a deep scarlet shawl draped around her shoulders. She was fleeing from a group of men carrying pitchforks. Each of them wore a symbol on their tunics in the region of the heart. It looked like some sort of tree. At the bottom of the painting, where the artist usually signed, were the same symbols Kelly had seen on all the artefacts: the three concentric circles and the battleaxe. Kelly had read the *Da Vinci Code* enough times to know to look behind the painting. But there was nothing to see. Nevertheless, going on a hunch, she ran her hands over the stones at various angles but came up with nothing. She then tapped on each section meticulously – listening for a hollow sound. Sure enough, she heard the telltale sound of a hidden panel. Kelly almost missed it as it was practically invisible – blending into the stone feature wall seamlessly.

Gotcha! she murmured. *But where is the keyhole?* Kelly ran her fingers over every inch of the stone facade until she found a well-camouflaged cap, covering the keyhole, toward the bottom of the panel.

Bingo! Kelly could scarcely contain her excitement at this new discovery and could not wait to see what lay inside the secret locker. The key fit perfectly. Turning the key in the lock, Kelly heard a resounding click as the lock gave way. She gently opened the panel and, using her cell phone torch, peered eagerly into the secret little locker. It contained a sort of journal and an ancient-looking scroll. Kelly carefully removed these items from the locker before closing the panel and replacing the keyhole cover.

She remembered seeing a tube case in the study. She placed the scroll into the tube and placed the journal into a clear plastic bag.

Before leaving the villa, Kelly realised that this would be her one chance to confirm – once and for all – if the Santiagos were allies or enemies. She grabbed the spare keys from the board and crept her way into the pool house. The Santiagos kept an immaculate place. The furniture was neat, albeit well-worn, with well-matched drapes and accessories in a sunset palette that matched the colour of the house.

Kelly headed to the desk at the corner of the bedroom, where she found the usual letters and bills, medical reports, and all sorts of folders in a well-organised drawer. The last drawer at the bottom of the column of drawers was locked. But Kelly was not about to prise it open with a steak knife. So she did a cursory sweep around the bedroom. A few antique jewellery boxes lay on the dresser. There were two containing women's jewellery and two containing men's jewellery – mainly watches and cufflinks – and a beautiful pin of a tree.

Where have I seen this symbol before? Oh, yes. I saw it in the painting in the master bedroom of the main house.

She snapped off a picture of the pin and, not wanting to spend any more time at the villa alone, Kelly quickly locked up and went back to the flat with its new front door. She figured it would be too dangerous to discuss anything over the phone, so Kelly tried to be patient and spent her time trying to find the meaning of the symbols on the artworks instead.

After a futile, hours-long search, Kelly gave up. Sheer boredom prompted her to carefully page through the journal. Of course, it was written entirely in that same ancient script as everything else they had discovered so far. But toward the end, in what appeared to be some sort of glossary or appendix, she saw a list of symbols or runes. The three concentric circles and the battleaxe were among them. *Finally, we are getting somewhere. Dimitri will have his work cut out for him tomorrow,* thought Kelly, smiling to herself.

12

Thugs and Prophecies

Kelly spent a rather tense day at the office. Try as she might, she could not will the hours to pass quickly enough. Dimitri had lectures and tutorials all morning and would only get a chance to meet in the early afternoon, which meant that she had to pretend that there were no significant developments to discuss. She felt like an insect under a microscope as Camilla kept a close eye on her all morning. She and Andie were feeling somewhat guilty, and responsible to some extent, for all the dangerous things that had suddenly been happening to Kelly.

"So I told Ronaldo that just because I have not dated anyone else the whole time I have been seeing him, he shouldn't now start taking liberties and acting like we are a steady couple or anything. You know what, Kelly? I think I am going to go out with someone else just to show him that it is really just casual between us – what do you think?" Camilla was on a rant about how Ronaldo was getting a swollen head because they had been exclusive for about three months and he thought it would become permanent.

"But haven't you ever fallen in love, Camilla? You know, had a steady relationship for a long time?" asked Kelly, curious about how this bombshell managed to evade being tied down to some wealthy royal or someone influential like that.

"Once. Just once. And I don't want to talk about it. Thank you very much. Case closed," she asserted. Camilla went strangely quiet for a while after that, and Kelly knew better than to push the matter.

"I guess I will have to get you raging drunk before you'll tell me. So, we will have to plan another ladies' sleepover soon." But Camilla barely managed a ghost of a smile, so Kelly dropped the subject altogether.

Besides, there was too much paperwork to wade through before she could traipse off to meet Dimitri. After what felt like a week of watching paint dry, it was finally time to head off to the university. Luckily, Camilla had to meet a client at the beach and would not be back for the rest of the day.

Dimitri was completely astounded by all the new information. "How did you manage to get your hands on all of this?" he asked incredulously.

"I don't know, maybe it's the witch in me – you know – witch's instinct and all," she joked.

They started with the scroll, which was written in archaic Navarro-Aragonese. "This is some sort of prophecy, as far as I can tell," mused Dimitri, fascinated by the artefact.

"Do you think you can translate it?" asked Kelly excitedly. Finally, some progress, she thought.

"Alright, from what I can manage to translate, it says something like this:

"The power of the Goddess; the giver of life; she imbued the flesh of her flesh with the secret art of healing, which shall forever live on through her bloodline until such time the line shall end. The last vessel of the Goddess shall return to the seat of this prophecy; Her gift from the Tree of Life shall give health, power, and victory to whomsoever she deems worthy.

"I don't know if I got the wording right but, this is a close approximation. The language is pretty tricky. No pun intended, dear witch," snickered Dimitri, and they both laughed uncontrollably.

"Okay, so the prophecy mentions the Tree of Life. In the painting, I saw a bunch of men in tunics chasing the woman that had to have been Paula de Eguiluz. And they had a sort of tree painted on their tunics. When I broke into the Santiagos' place at the villa – yeah, you can judge me all you want. Just chalk it up to my witch's instinct, will you? Anyway, I found a pin with that same tree on it. What do you think it means?" asked Kelly, wondering why the men who were attacking Paula in the painting had the same symbol alluded to in the prophecy.

"Perhaps they felt that Paula and the prophecy were going against the church, and they wanted to protect the faith of the people or something. I can't speculate. But let us look at the journal for more answers before we can hazard a reasonable guess, shall we?"

"Spoken like a wise professor, indeed. Alright, let's take a look at the journal."

"This is the original notebook of Paula de Eguiluz! It says that she has placed a charm on it so that it will survive until the last daughter in her line gets to read her life's work! And that could very well be you, Kelly! I, I feel so privileged to be able to help you read the work of your early ancestor," he babbled, utterly awestruck.

"Thank you for all the help, Dimitri. This means so much to me; you've no idea." Kelly's excitement was palpable but she knew there was still a long road ahead. She didn't place much stock in the supernatural, nor was she especially religious. Kelly's motto in life was simple. Be good, do good, and see the good in others. It wasn't exactly a profound philosophy, but it was the sum total of her belief system – her recent forays into breaking and entering revealed her flexibility on even these simple principles.

"Well, the journal includes her most prized recipes for tonics and elixirs. It is more of a medical journal with a smattering of recorded life events. Oh, there is a note to her future daughters. It is a letter to you, actually, Kelly. This is what it says – a rough translation:

"My dearest daughter of the future,

"I hope that you are also a healer and that female healers are treated more kindly in your time. To ensure the protection of my line, I have had to create a few ways to ensure that we survive when all others like myself have been burned.

"The elixir of eternal life is a hoax, yet many will seek it. I have retired to distant shores, outrunning my enemies and assuming a new identity for my newborn daughter and myself after the tragic loss of her father – the love of my life.

"Our lineage will have to remain hidden as those who seek power will stop at nothing to find us. The group of thugs calling themselves the 'Cazadores de la Bruja Poderosa' – or 'Hunters of the Mighty Witch' – will stop at nothing to wipe out our lineage or force us to give them the elixir of eternal life. They have arrogantly chosen the Tree of Life as their symbol and believe that we really are witches instead of healers. They ascribe some sort of otherworldly power to us when, in truth, it is just knowledge of healing arts and herbs that they could also learn if they tried. It is a foolishness for which I will not die – nor will any of my descendants.

"I have entrusted a few people with the truth: the prophecy is a lie concocted by those who would seek to destroy my lineage. Take extra care, dear daughter, and be assured that I will be protecting you from the great beyond.

"With love,

"Your Healing Mother

"Paula de Eguiluz"

They sat in shocked silence for a while. Kelly read the written translation of Paula's message a few times.

At last, Kelly spoke. Outrage gave her voice a grating edge. "So this tree gang is out to kill me because of some grudge someone had over my long-dead ancestor? Or worse, maybe they are after the damned elixir of life, and they think that I will somehow know how to make it, seeing as how I am the last living daughter in Paula's line? Oh my gosh! That's right. Lenny doesn't have any kids, Aunt Judy didn't have any either, and I am already thirty-six years old. It isn't likely that I will settle down and raise a family at my age. Which means that I am the last daughter who is somehow supposed to have the recipe to this elixir of eternal life! What a crock of shite!" Kelly's cheeks had turned crimson with outrage, and her breathing had grown ragged.

"So, this whole time, these tree men have been hunting me down. Maybe they were not sure if I am, in fact, the last daughter. Or maybe they don't have all the key information. Or wait, maybe one of these recipes IS called the Elixir of Life and that is what they've been looking for this whole time!" Kelly was thinking out loud and began rambling.

"It seems like there are lots of elixir recipes here. Oh, this one is called the Elixir of Gold, Victory, and Power. It could be the one they're after," suggested Dimitri.

"Alright, Prof, please go ahead and translate these recipes for me after I've scanned every page in case it disintegrates or goes missing," recommended Kelly.

"By the way, can you tell me what the two symbols on all the artefacts mean? I noticed a glossary of them on the last pages of the journal..." she asked.

"Ah, yes. This one that looks like a ripple with the three rings – it means Truth. And that axe actually means protector. So it means—"

"Protector of the Truth! Cool! Thanks, Prof."

"In the meantime, I need to dig up all I can about these Tree Thugs or 'Hunters of the Mighty Witch' or whatever they're calling themselves these days. Unbelievable!" she fumed. "It really gets my goat that they'd been working for Aunt Judy, right under her nose for years! I bet the Santiagos had something to do with her death! I need to tell Andie and Camilla about this so we can work on a plan to catch these thugs before they fill in their missing pieces and come after me for real."

Kelly paused and faced Dimitri, looking him squarely in the eyes. She placed her hands on his shoulders and said, "Dimitri, I know that I am asking a lot from you. But I need you to not tell a soul about what we've learned. At least until these thugs are taken care of and it is safe for us to tell the real story of the Legend of Paula de Eguiluz and her Daughters." Kelly did a theatrical flourish at the end.

"But seriously, Dimitri. I think we've got a group of cut-throat cult types on our hands, and who knows what strange legend they've concocted about this prophecy nonsense? We don't even know who's involved with these hooligans. I mean, look at how the Santiagos managed to insinuate themselves into working at the villa..." Her voice trailed off at the thought that even Dimitri could be one of them. "You're not one of the tree thugs, are you, Dimitri? Oh my gosh! Your name even ends in 'tree'!" she mocked, and they had a good and much-needed laugh.

"I think you're barking up the wrong tree there, bruja," chuckled Dimitri, and then growing serious again, he added, "Don't worry,

Kelly. I assure you, I am quite an agnostic. I have no interest in the metaphysical, even though I spend most of my time studying those who believed."

13

The List

"I call to order the meeting of this sacred coven of the sisterhood of the last daughter of Paula de Eguiluz!" Kelly announced in her most ominous voice. "Just kidding!" She laughed as she sat with her confidantes, Andie and Camilla, around the dinner table at what had become their headquarters – Camilla's house. Being on the edge of town, it gave them greater privacy and was large enough to accommodate them comfortably.

The trio enjoyed a quick dinner of Rioja-style chicken with garlic and peppers, spicy *patatas bravas,* and a crunchy salad. Churros and thick drinking chocolate rounded it off on a note of decadence. They soon settled down to their roundtable conference. Kelly gave them a rundown of everything she had been up to and all that she had discovered with the help of Professor Dimitri Vázquez.

"I will run a background check on the Santiagos and, with your permission, Kelly, I will also have to do a check on your boyfriend too," said Andie, mildly apologetic.

"FYI, he is not my boyfriend! But go ahead. I think we can't afford to take any chances right now," admitted Kelly, a bit on edge.

"We will have to find out what this 'Tree Gang' of witch-hunters is all about and what exactly it is that they're after. Do you think you could pull some strings at MI6, Andie?" Camilla was visibly shaken by the possibility that Kelly could be in very real danger.

"What really baffles me is whether the thefts of the artefacts have anything to do with the prophecy, or are they a separate act of some criminal mastermind or other?" Kelly said pensively.

"We are asking the right questions. Now we have to seek the right answers," replied Andie.

"Tell you what, Kelly. Let me take over from here. You have done a bang-up job of sleuthing, despite all our warnings, might I add?" She paused to give Kelly an appropriately critical look even though she was, inwardly, quite impressed by the younger woman.

"Shouldn't we alert the local authorities about the thugs?" asked Camilla, concerned about their safety, especially Kelly's.

"I think we should wait until we have more information to share. For now, confidentiality is our closest ally. We don't know how far or how widely this organisation extends. And until we do, we should tread carefully," cautioned Andie.

"So, you're suggesting we pretend as if it's business as usual, then?" asked Camilla, doubt evident on her face.

"Well, at least until we have more intel, of course," explained Andie.

"I think we need to re-examine our list of persons of interest and investigate them more actively. And we should move the Santiagos to the top of that list too," recommended Kelly.

"Agreed. Let's meet again once we've got something solid to go on. Until then, we go about our normal lives. Except – Kelly, I strongly recommend that you not go anywhere alone, please," asserted Andie, taking Kelly by the shoulders to reinforce her message.

"I have no doubt in my mind now that our dear friend Judy was murdered. And I intend to get to the bottom of this! I promise you,

Kelly – we will find those bastards who killed your Aunt Judy, and they will pay for it."

Three days after the trio of women met at Camilla's house, Andie called another meeting. They met in the dead of night, and Andie swept the place for bugs or other types of listening devices. She also activated a gadget she called a white noise generator to run 'interference' in the event that someone was still listening via external listening devices.

"Wow, Andie. Paranoid or what?" joked Kelly, but she was grateful to Andie for being so thorough.

"I am not taking any more chances. You will understand why when you hear what I managed to glean from our two very special guests and the local interrogation centre," began Andie.

"Say again?" asked Kelly, not sure she liked where this was heading.

"Never mind how we acquired it. The important thing is that we managed to gain some valuable intel on the band of thugs who call themselves *Cazadores de la Bruja Poderosa*, or 'The Hunters of the Mighty Witch'. It took a lot of gentle persuading, if you know what I mean. He refused to give up the ringleader or name names, even upon the threat of death. You've gotta give the slippery bastard credit for loyalty," admitted Andie.

"So, you captured and detained the Santiagos?" asked Kelly, suddenly feeling a bit queasy. *I did this. This is all my fault.*

"Before you go beating yourself up about this, Kelly, you should listen to what we found out," cautioned Andie, raising her palms in a stop signal.

"We?" asked Camilla.

"Yes, I have had to call in an interrogation specialist – fluent in Spanish. He is a trustworthy ally whose identity I cannot disclose to you. I'm sure you understand. We don't know who is in on this thuggery, and it is safe to say we need to proceed with extreme caution. By the way, I had your boyfriend" – catching Kelly's warning look, she amended it to – "I mean Professor Dimitri Vázquez thoroughly checked out, and he is squeaky clean, except for a few unpaid speeding tickets, that is."

"Good to know." Kelly's small smile was bashful.

"Unfortunately, I can't say the same about Señor Andrés Santiago. He was born into the organisation and seems to be some sort of lieutenant in the ranks. He is wanted for breaking and entering out in Madrid, and his name came up at Interpol on smuggling charges – he brought in some valuable artefacts from the Dominican Republic a few years back. So you can stop feeling guilty about us bringing him in, Kelly. He isn't the man you think he is. In fact, the woman posing as his wife isn't even his wife at all but another member of the Tree Gang!" Andie had worked herself into a mini-tantrum.

"Okay, Andie. I will try to make peace with it. Thank you," conceded Kelly.

"Santiago is a real piece of work, ladies," continued Andie. "His mission was to secure the journal and original prophecy, rumoured to be somewhere in the villa. Once it had been confirmed that Judy Fargo was one of Paula's daughters, she became a target of this mob, which is why she decided to stop travelling back and forth and relocate permanently to Spain. To throw them off the scent of her niece. As far as they knew, Judy was the last in Paula's line of daughters," explained Andie, dejectedly.

"Oh, my gosh! I was so mean to her about moving here. I accused her of not loving us and wanting to escape the responsibility of being a mum to Lenny and me. Even said such hurtful things to her," lamented Kelly. They took a short break while Kelly gathered herself.

Camilla made a round of hot chocolate, and they sat for a while, just taking in all the new information. Kelly extolled the virtues of Aunt Judy, sharing random childhood memories she kept locked within her heart of hearts. It was a full forty-five minutes before Andie picked up the thread of her story once again.

"Getting back to Santiago. Beset by cataracts and failing vision, which he neglected to admit to the organisation, Santiago had been unable to fulfil his mission until you did it for him, Kelly. But your flat had been ransacked on his instructions the very afternoon you arrived at the villa with Dimitri. They thought that you may have already found it on your first visit to the villa when the Santiagos were not on the property," explained Andie, clearly outraged that they would be so brazen as to break into Kelly's flat.

"Unbelievable! Those devious old codgers do not deserve my sympathy. You were right, Andie. Go on," replied Kelly in disgust. She felt less guilty about breaking into the pool house after hearing how easy it was for them to sanction the same invasion of her own space.

"Wait!" interrupted Camilla, curiosity getting the better of her. "Is any of this linked to the artefact robberies at all, Andie?"

"In a way, yes. You see, whoever is leading this rabble wants to gain absolute power. These folks have their own beliefs around the extent of Paula's powers. From what I understand, the founder of this group was a Catholic priest who had been excommunicated from the church for turning to Paula for help with a severe case of oedema or some such affliction. She healed him completely within a matter of days, yet he had been suffering with the condition for years," explained Andie, proudly.

"So, what – as a show of his gratitude, he gathered a mob of farmers with pitchforks to hunt her down? Wow!" Kelly's reaction was filled with acid.

"He lost his marbles when the church kicked him out, and he blamed Paula. Suddenly, Paula became the scapegoat for anything untoward that happened in the area. But that is not the most astounding part of the story." Andie paused for effect, and both Camilla and Kelly leaned forward, holding their breath in anticipation.

"Okay, skip to the good part. We can always circle back to the details later. Go on," whispered Camilla, nodding enthusiastically.

"These so-called witch hunters have their own understanding of the prophecy. According to their beliefs, only the last daughter of Paula de Eguiluz will inherit the full might of Paula's powers. She alone will have the power to create the elixir from the Tree of Life, and the person who drinks this potion will be victorious, wealthy beyond measure, and wield absolute power and dominion over whomever he chooses. If he manages to amass the entire collection of artefacts believed to have been the property of Paula de Eguiluz, their power, according to the legend, will become amplified. You see, they believe that before she died, Paula placed a large portion of her powers into the objects in her collection and only the last daughter will be able to activate those powers." Andie burst into laughter and the others joined her. It sounded much too ludicrous to them.

"That sounds ridiculous, especially when you say it out loud like that," snorted Camilla.

"I can't believe that this cult or whatever has been going on for centuries!" hooted Kelly, wiping away the tears of laughter from her streaming face until a sobering thought struck her. "I wonder why they didn't make off with Aunt Judy's collection?" she mused.

"I suppose that would have been one of the last steps, after all the other information had been gathered," suggested Andie haltingly, trying to reason it out in her mind as she spoke.

"Or, perhaps, a certain eccentric someone who has been after the property for years is actually the leader of this strange cult!" murmured Camilla.

"Diego Reyes!" they both shouted at once.

"That's it!" Kelly burst out. "I have an idea of how we can suss out the leader of the Tree Gang!"

"Uh-oh. Should we be worried?" groaned Camilla, exchanging glances with Andie.

"Look, whoever is behind all the robberies is trying to amass every last piece in Paula's extensive collection. By now, they must suspect that I am the last daughter in Paula's lineage, which is why they have been so busy. Our list of suspects includes Diego Reyes; Mateo Hernández, the antiques dealer; the Duque Carlos Miguel Luis; and Isabella Ruiz, the history lady, right?"

"Right..." replied Andie, trying to follow Kelly's idea closely.

"So, what if our list of suspects is inaccurate? Or what if we are on the money? Either way, how do we bag the leader before they do some serious damage around here?"

"What are you planning, Kelly?" asked Camilla apprehensively. She did not like where Kelly was going with this.

"I think I should host an auction of Aunt Judy's private collection. We can highlight that the private journal of Paula de Eguiluz will be the event's showstopper. It will be widely advertised, and we can set up an elaborate surveillance and security crew strategically positioned to swoop in on the culprit when they try to kill or nab me. As the hostess of the event, I will obviously be an unmissable target—"

"No way! I don't like it – not one tiny bit!" burst Andie, shaking her head dismissively.

"I swear I will not be in any kind of danger the whole time, Andie. We can't let them catch us off guard. I say we deal with these thugs on our own terms. Let them come to us instead of us walking into some trap of their devising. We have to be proactive if we hope to catch them. Meanwhile, I will study up on this Tree of Life business and Dimitri's translations so that – should I be taken – I will at least be able to convince these thugs that I can make the elixir they're after. Camilla, do you have an idea of where we can have this auction? We will have to hire out the venue well in advance to put the plan into place. It will work, Andie. You know it is the only way we can know for sure who is behind all of these thefts. And who knows? Maybe we will find Aunt Judy's killer at the same time too."

"I don't know. We will have to work out the feasibility, including all the risks and factoring in all the permutations of how the events can unfold. I am not saying 'yes'. I'm saying 'maybe'. Are we on the same page, Kelly?" asserted Andie, in full MI6 mode.

14

A Grand Plan

"According to what I could dig up about this Tree of Life, it is actually the yew tree that is used in loads of medical treatments today, including ovarian and breast cancer treatments. It contains a large concentration of the alkaloid taxol, which has been found to be effective in the fight against these cancers," reported Kelly in fascination.

She and Dimitri were trying to gather as much research as they could find about each of the artefacts, ingredients, and recipes in Paula's journal.

"I mean, did you know that several faiths and ancient civilisations believed in the Tree of Life? There is a Celtic version that connected the Earth, sky, and tree. It was called the *Crann Bethadh* and had a wide trunk with many branches that swirled into a Celtic pattern to meet the sky above, while the root extended into the earth and then met the pattern above so that the entire tree was depicted as a circular symbol. Then, in Christianity, the first and last chapters of the Bible mention the Tree of Life. Some say that there are actually two trees – the Tree of Life and the Tree of Knowledge, and others say that they are one and the same. The Egyptians, Hindus, Buddhists, Jews, and even Muslims have this sacred tree somewhere in their belief systems. Even the Mesoamerican and Norse cultures believed in it!"

"That really is quite profound. I thought that perhaps it was a symbol of a particular type of healing tree or something. But now, perhaps it is more of a universal symbol of harmony, rejuvenation, and peace."

"I think that both those viewpoints are valid, Dimitri. It doesn't necessarily have to be one and not the other," replied Kelly excitedly.

They studied on in companionable silence, and Kelly realised that she had come to value her time spent with this humble, good-humoured academic. She was really hoping that they would remain friends after all of this was over. *If we live through it,* she thought morbidly.

"The translation of Paula's journal is almost complete," reported Dimitri.

"Thank you so much, Dimitri. You've been such a wonderful help with all of this." She could feel her cheeks flush.

Kelly considered telling Dimitri about her plan, but she thought better of it – not wanting to place him in any danger. *Besides, the fewer people who know about what we're up to, the greater our chances of succeeding*, she thought grimly.

She set about gathering as much information on each artefact as she could in order to put together a plausible brochure. Camilla was left in charge of finding the best venue for the auction itself. She would consult with Andie on its suitability to set the trap and contain what they were hoping would be the ringleaders of the 'Tree Gang'. If all went as planned, they would bag the key players and hand them over to the authorities with enough evidence to put them away for a long time. And Kelly could live out her life without having a target on her back.

"It just blows my mind that people believe in occult powers and witches, prophecies, and magic," said Kelly, glowering.

"Yes, I suppose there are all types of folks in this world, like the flat Earthers and those that feed off of urban legends and myths and the wormhole cults – lots of strange beliefs are floating around these days," added Dimitri.

Kelly was relieved to hear that Dimitri didn't place any stock in magic or mystical powers. She promised to stay in touch and took her leave.

The most annoying part about this entire drama was that, as promised, Andie had placed a tail on Kelly. At least he was being discreet about it. Andie made certain that Kelly met Gustavo Costa, a rather bland-looking Portuguese man with a rather forgettable face. In this way, Kelly would be aware of who he was in the unfortunate event that anything untoward did happen or if the thugs decided to tail her themselves – which Andie suspected they'd been doing for some time now.

Returning to HQ – Camilla's place – everyone updated the team on their progress. "I think we've narrowed down the venue to two possible options, but I've got to get back to them by tomorrow. So, Andie, I was wondering if we could meet by about ten to take a look at the place?" asked Camilla.

"Sure, I will swing by the office, and we can shoot off to both venues before I meet with my intel guy for lunch," replied Andie amiably. Somehow, Kelly visualised the trio as the female version of The A-Team with Andie as the team leader, Hannibal. She giggled as she pictured Andie with a cigar in her mouth saying, "I love it when a plan comes together."

"Something funny, *bruja*?" asked Camilla jokingly.

"Just thinking of an old television series Lenny loved watching reruns of when we were kids," replied Kelly nostalgically.

"Are you sure you don't want to let Lenny know about what's going on, Kelly?" asked Camilla, concerned because they were usually stronger together – and Kelly's decision to leave him totally in the dark about this was gnawing at Camilla.

"He needs to focus on his own life with Laura. I don't want him worrying about me unnecessarily from across the channel when there really isn't anything he can do from there but work himself up into a ball of stress. No, we leave Lenny out of it, please," she affirmed.

"Okay. But there's still loads of time to change your mind anyway. Back to the plans. I have engaged the services of Señor Julio Javier, who is a masterful auctioneer. He will be here the day before so that we can go over the details of each piece and the order in which they will be auctioned," added Camilla.

"On that note, we will have to leave the journal for the end, and I will stay with it in the holding area, bringing it out when it's time," added Kelly with a sly smile.

"Right," cut in Andie. "I almost forgot to mention that I have arranged for every last artefact to be taken to a secure location. Once word of the auction goes public, it might scare the 'Tree Gang' into breaking into the villa to bag the artefacts, journal, and whatever else they can get their hands on before the event itself," explained Andie.

"That is a fantastic plan, Andie. But can you trust the people who will be housing them?" asked Kelly sceptically. She'd watched enough money heist movies in her time to know that valuables are most vulnerable when they are in transit.

"Luckily, our secure facility is located in a remote region with loads of discreet security measures in place," assured Andie.

"Well, I don't see how we can avoid the move. It is the smart thing to do. Thank you, Andie, for taking care of all the details," replied Kelly with a tone of resignation.

"Once we've decided on a venue, we will talk decor and catering," reminded Camilla, relieved that Judy's life insurance funds had come in just when they would be needing a fair bit of money to put the auction together.

"I've been reading through all the recipes and herbal remedies in Paula's journal. In the unlikely event that they do manage to capture me, I want to be able to convince them that I can make the elixir and dupe them until the cavalry arrives," admitted Kelly, her matter-of-fact tone coming across as very brave.

"Kelly! Stop thinking like that at once!" chided Camilla. "This is going to work, and you will be safe at all times, right, Andie? Tell her."

"Well, it wouldn't hurt to have a few countermeasures in place in case of the unexpected," muttered Andie. "I will see about what we can put together in case you are captured, Kelly. In fact, I think we should set something up well before then. Perhaps some sort of panic button."

Just then, Andie had to take a call and stepped onto the balcony. "So, what's the deal with you and the good Professor Vázquez?" teased Camilla, wiggling her eyebrows suggestively.

"Nothing!" replied Kelly defensively and a little too loudly. "Look, we're just friends, and we have been working well on our research, that's all, Camilla. So, lay off, okay?"

"Okay!" capitulated Camilla with her hands raised in surrender.

Andie rushed in and threw on her coat, muttering, "I've gotta dash. Something's come up. Kelly, it's getting late. Why don't you bunk with Camilla tonight?" Andie caught Camilla's eye.

"I think that is a wonderful idea, Kelly. You can help me work out an action plan. I wanna teach that smug Ronaldo a lesson," explained Camilla determinedly.

"I'm gonna have to pass on your offer this time, Camilla. Sorry. I have some studying to do but I will be fine, you two, don't worry. I have a burly bodyguard to keep me safe," said Kelly with a smile.

"Alright, I didn't want to tell you this, Kelly. But Dimitri was attacked and beaten up," admitted Andie.

"What!" exclaimed Kelly and Camilla at once.

"Please stay put while we get to the bottom of this," threw Andie over her shoulder on her way out.

"No way, I'm coming with you, Andie. This is appalling! I have to see him. This is all my fault!" said Kelly, cringing and feeling queasy at the notion that she had endangered his life.

Andie turned around, took a deep breath, and spoke patiently. "Trust me, Kelly. I know how you feel, but you coming to see him at the police station is only going to confirm that you were working with him. We don't know who will be watching the station. Sorry, hun. I will call as soon as I know more, I promise." Andie gave Kelly a warm hug before dashing off.

"Come on back inside, Kel. He will be alright, I am sure of it. We will wait for Andie's call."

"I can't wait for these thugs to be behind bars, Camilla," fumed Kelly.

She tried to study the translation of Paula's journal, but her thoughts were all over the place. So she gave up trying and took to pacing in Camilla's guest room until she received a text message from

Andie to say that all was well. They'd agreed to not send out any detailed information via cell phone.

In the morning, Andie brought breakfast, and the shaken trio sat down to chat. "Like we suspected, the 'Tree Gang' had you followed to the university a few times. They knew that you were protected, Kelly, so they waited for you to leave before moving in on Dimitri."

"That is just diabolical. Poor Dimitri. Was he badly hurt, Andie?" asked Kelly. Her voice sounded strangled as she was livid about the thugs and worried about Dimitri while struggling with her intense feelings of guilt.

"They did work him over some, but he is a strong lad – for a bookworm, that is," admitted Andie, not meeting Kelly's searching eyes.

"Luckily, he had given you every shred of material he had been working on, and he kept no electronic copies either. He was really smart to do that because they wanted to know why you had been visiting him so often. At first, he pretended that you were his girlfriend, whom he was tutoring in Spanish. But that didn't fly with them."

Kelly blushed in spite of herself. "So, what happened next?" she prompted. She felt a lump in her throat.

"They threatened him and when that didn't work, they beat him up. I am so sorry."

Kelly, trembling with rage and guilt, spoke in an almost unrecognisable voice. "These bastards are going to pay for all the destruction they have been wreaking all over Spain. I – Is Dimitri in the hospital, Andie?"

"He had to go into casualty – to check for broken ribs and to get a few stitches. Relax. He is fine, Kelly," Andie said, reaching out to grab Kelly's arm to steady her.

"I am just glad that he is okay. Andie, I hate to ask, but did they force any information out of him?" asked Camilla, somewhat concerned about the mission as much as she was worried about Dimitri.

"I was worried about that too. But he told them that he was teaching Kelly about Spanish history and the language, and that was all he claimed to know, even after a sound beating. Realising it was a dead end, they threatened him and left him with a number to call if she ever asked him to do any document translations for her. And then they left," reported Andie.

"A number? That is great news! Your team can trace it back to the owner, right?" asked Kelly. A ray of hope flitted across her face.

"We tried that already, but it is a burner phone, so we reached a dead end with that. These guys are smart, and I wouldn't be at all surprised if some of them have had military training. We should not underestimate these people. And whoever is funding this operation has money to burn. That's for certain," concluded Andie bitterly.

"Well, all four of our suspects are very wealthy. It could be any one of them. Or maybe they are working together as part of a larger operation," suggested Camilla, grimacing as her imagination ran through all the possibilities.

"Kelly, I know that you are going to want to see Dimitri, but he asked that you not do that," said Andie gently.

"Oh my gosh! He hates me, doesn't he?" wailed Kelly.

"No, no, no! It is nothing like that, Kelly. He just wants you to be safe. He feels like they are watching his every move now, and they could ambush you if you stop by his office again. He wants you to be careful, and I couldn't agree more," said Andie, taking Kelly by the shoulders.

The next few days were a flurry of activity as the trio finalised all the arrangements for the auction. The artefacts from the villa were safely transferred to the secure facility without a hitch, and all security protocols had been fully engaged.

As a matter of urgency, Andie arranged for Kelly to carry a panic button in her purse or pocket that would alert both herself and Gustavo Costa that she was in trouble. They performed some tests of the device's effectiveness and range, but sadly, they found it to have a limited range of only 300 metres, which meant that in most instances, only Gustavo would be able to intercept the alert. But Andie was confident that Gustavo Costa would be able to handle any situation that arose, as she had worked with him on previous missions when she was still in the service of MI6.

Andie and Camilla selected the Royal Contessa Hotel in Almería City as the venue for the auction. They booked the entire conference centre so as to have full control over what happened and to accommodate both the artefacts and security personnel comfortably. The entrances and exits seemed manageable, and the hotel was fully equipped to cater to their needs, providing the appropriate level of class and sophistication to attract both the nouveau riche and aristocracy alike.

Camilla was in her element as she dived headlong into the decor and catering arrangements. Judy's good friend and banker, Alex Stransky, would take care of the tickets, billing, and proceeds from the auction. Alex was part German and part Russian, but his family had moved to Spain several decades ago, and he spoke Spanish fluently despite his strange accent.

"I think it is high time we paid each of our suspects a visit. You know, to extend them a personal invitation to the event and feel them out," suggested Kelly conspiratorially.

"Sounds good. I'm in," agreed Camilla despite the long list of things she still had to get done. She would not let Kelly take that on by herself.

15

The Event

Their first stop was Isabella Ruiz – local historian and the exceedingly wealthy president of the Spanish Heritage Preservation Society in Almería. This geriatric minx was as feisty as she was shrewd, and Kelly was really glad that Camilla had agreed to accompany her on these visits. Being something of an introvert, Kelly always entered social scenes with trepidation, but thanks to Camilla, she was improving.

"Ah. To what do I owe the honour of this visit, Señorita Simpson?" asked Isabella in her tittering voice that immediately set Kelly's teeth on edge.

"We brought you a little gift," announced Camilla in her most charming tone, and she punctuated it with a dazzling smile. At the last minute, they had dashed off to Señora Alba's kitchen for her famous almond biscuits that were to die for.

"And we are here to personally invite you to grace our private auction at the Royal Contessa Hotel in Almería City. The event will take place in a week from now on Friday, February thirteenth. All the details are on the invitation, Señora Ruiz," said Kelly with an ingratiating smile.

"So, it is true, then? Are you really in possession of the legendary collection of Paula de Eguiluz?" asked Isabella sceptically after studying the invitation.

"There is only one way for you to find out, Señora Ruiz." Kelly finished off with a sweet smile.

"I would very much prefer to have a private viewing of the collection before I can commit to attending this event, if you don't mind," replied Isabella, her voice dripping with a mix of condescension and superiority.

"If only that were possible, señora. Unfortunately, due to the recent spate of artefact thefts in the area, we have had to hire a private security company to house the collection in their vaults until the auction. So, we are unable to fulfil your request at this time," explained Camilla with her smile still fixed in place.

I wonder if Camilla's face hurts as much as mine does right now. This constant smiling is very hard work! thought Kelly ruefully.

"But we would still be most appreciative if you would attend the event. We promise that the banquet and ambience alone will make for a delightful evening in themselves, even if you don't quite like any of the pieces on offer. Although that would be hard to imagine," added Kelly, trying to mimic Camilla's effortless grace.

"Yes, well..." began the old woman as she scanned Kelly from top to bottom and back again with unmasked disdain. Kelly was tempted to sniff under her armpits and clothing in front of Isabella, but she tried to be on her best behaviour regardless of what the old coot said or did.

"Ah! Friday the thirteenth? Was that deliberate or coincidental?" asked Isabella with a light-hearted titter.

Talk about being bipolar! There are pills for that, you know? Thought Kelly. Her mind was out of control as she struggled to keep the reins on her responses, so she let Camilla wrap this one up.

"It was purely coincidental, I assure you, Señora Ruiz. It was the only date available within our timeframe," answered Camilla, infusing an air of mystery into her tone.

"Well, I might swing by if I am feeling sociable and generous. Thank you for stopping by and for the, um... biscuits." She held the beautiful gift pack of biscuits by the tip with her index finger and thumb, as if it were a soiled nappy, uttering the last word with as much distaste as she could muster into a single word.

"You are most welcome, Señora Ruiz. And we look forward to enjoying your lively company at the auction on the thirteenth. Adiós."

Back in the safety of the car, Kelly couldn't help but comment on their experience. "What a snooty bitch! How did you manage to remain so gracious, Camilla?"

"It's a gift, I know. But we have bigger problems. If the old dowager blabs that we invited her before inviting the Duque, it will be viewed as a breach of etiquette, and he might not attend on principle. Shit! How could I have been so stupid?" she chastised herself while reaching for her cell phone in the hopes of repairing the damage before anyone was the wiser.

Speaking rapidly in Spanish, Camilla tried to secure an audience with the Duque, but he was indisposed. However, his assistant agreed to accept the invitation on his behalf. So Camilla emailed the invitation to the Duque's PA and hoped for the best. "Let's see if we get an RSVP from his office before the end of this week. Fingers crossed chiquita," Camilla said with a smile, crossing her perfectly manicured, sinewy fingers and then giving Kelly's arm a squeeze.

"I think we should give them a follow-up call before the RSVPs are due, just as a reminder," suggested Kelly.

"Sure. I was planning to do that with all those who may have forgotten to RSVP. I love it when we're on the same page. Next stop – the offices of my dear pompous friend, Diego Reyes," announced Camilla with mock enthusiasm while, alongside her, Kelly groaned dramatically.

While calling Reyes Enterprises, Camilla was placed on hold for a full ten minutes, during which time she had already driven halfway to the city. Eventually, she was transferred to Reyes's secretary, who said that they would try to squeeze them between his scheduled appointments if Camilla was prepared to wait awhile. Camilla agreed, knowing that she would not be easily forgiven if she neglected to invite Diego in person.

Entering the offices of Diego Reyes, Kelly felt like they were stepping into another world. A kaleidoscopic miasma of garish artwork and tapestries lined the bright tangerine-coloured walls, with a smattering of large potted plants and vines haphazardly interspersed between them. The secretary was a transgender person wearing a dress shirt and tie with a multicoloured frilly micro-mini, electric blue fishnet leggings, and purple spike-heeled knee-high boots. At least they were courteous enough to stand up to greet the pair, showing off their well-formed, never-ending legs. Their bangles tinkled noisily as Kelly and Camilla were directed to the waiting area.

They found themselves in a lounge with a set of velvety blue couches; a huge pink, yellow, and orange lava lamp; and a variety of other Flower Power paraphernalia in a rather kitsch mishmash that soon began to hurt Kelly's eyes. In a short space of time, though, they inwardly extolled the comfort of the sofas with gratitude, since it was a full three hours until they were shown into the great business tycoon's office. Kelly regretted not bothering with breakfast that morning and gave her tummy a self-conscious squeeze as it protested loudly. Just when she was about to break open the pack of biscuits, in desperation, the secretary came back to usher them into Diego's office.

"Camilla López," he greeted cheerfully, taking Camilla's hand to give it a chivalrous peck. "It is wonderful to see you again, Señorita Simpson. To what do I owe this rare honour?" He wore a psychedelic cravat with an amethyst jewel at the centre and a bright cerise-coloured suit with a pair of black and white brogue shoes to match his black cane with its large, pink bejewelled head.

"I felt really badly about the way we parted ways when you came to see me at my office. So, I brought you a little peace offering and an opportunity to join our elite private auction. You see, my late aunt had amassed a sizeable collection that had once belonged to Paula de Eguiluz. And I have no intention of holding onto the collection. So, I have decided to host a private auction to ensure that the pieces find suitable homes," explained Kelly.

"Do you really have the collection of the infamous and notorious witch, Paula de Eguiluz?" asked Diego incredulously.

"Why don't you come and find out on the evening of the thirteenth of February?" asked Camilla, smiling coquettishly.

"Is it a Friday, by any chance?" asked the businessman, jokingly.

"As a matter of fact, it is!" replied Camilla. She knew how much men preened when women laughed at their jokes.

"Well! In that case, of course, I will come. Thank you for the invitation, señoritas. Please leave the details with my secretary, Juan-ita. But I will take the biscuits, thank you." He smiled good-naturedly.

They took a much-needed lunch break at Cocina Valenciana, Camilla's go-to place in Almería. After they were seated comfortably in a cosy booth with soft leather upholstery, Kelly admitted, "I really like him and hope he turns out to be a good guy." They had to be very cautious about what they said when they were out in the open.

"I don't trust anyone. And you shouldn't either, Kelly. We're dealing with a bunch of ruthless savages, and we need to tread very carefully indeed. Besides, men like Diego seldom get to where they are in life without blurring some lines. Remember that," whispered Camilla, in earnest. That warning made Kelly's skin crawl because she knew that there was a ring of truth to what she'd said.

Just then, Señora Álvarez, the chef, came over to check on how they were doing, and Camilla asked her for the recipe for her famous fideuà, which they had enjoyed immensely. It was a Spanish vermicelli dish, which she prepared with a unique blend of spices and an assortment of seafood, from clams to prawns to calamari, and garnished it with fresh herbs, creating a unique and scrumptious culinary experience that had patrons coming back for more. And after the day they were having, some almond cake and custard were the perfect way to fortify themselves for the last leg of their mission.

"Are you ready to visit the last person on our list, Kelly?" asked Camilla, scarcely able to move.

"To be honest, I think I might need a long siesta after this heavy meal. But, yeah, let's get this over and done with," replied Kelly sluggishly.

Their next visit was with Mateo Hernández, the antiques dealer, who travelled extensively. Camilla phoned the store in advance to arrange a meeting with Mateo via his efficient and introverted sister, Carmen. Unfortunately, Mateo was spending the week off the grid and would only get back to the shop in three days. "He sure is a man of mystery, isn't he?" commented Kelly, irritably.

"So, what shall we do about the invitation?" mused Camilla.

"Hey, let's go visit Carmen anyway. I have been meaning to visit the antiques store ever since we met the night of the Bread Festival, but I haven't had a chance," suggested Kelly optimistically.

"Oh, do you mean the local cat burglars and witch hunters have been keeping you busy have they?" mocked Camilla as she set a course for the store, Adornos Antiguos – roughly translated as 'vintage ornaments' – owned and run by the Hernández family.

The store was the kind of place you could spend days in without realising you'd invested so much of your time. The antiques were clearly well cared for, and they were masterfully displayed to bring out the beauty of each piece. Kelly was grateful that she went there with Camilla. Had she gone alone, she would have left with a boot full of decorative yet useless knick-knacks and an empty purse. She was especially interested in an exquisitely crafted candlestick holder, made from wrought iron, in the shape of the Tree of Life. In fact, she let out a soft gasp the moment she laid eyes on it.

"It is a beautiful piece from the fifteenth century," began a slightly built woman with long tresses of chestnut hair and caramel-coloured eyes that seemed to have glowing lanterns burning inside them.

"Are you Carmen?" asked Kelly, hesitantly.

"Sí. ¿Cómo está usted?" she asked politely in a low, throaty voice that didn't match her slight figure in the least. Camilla took over the conversation in Spanish, urging her to either attend the auction herself or ensure that Mateo didn't miss it, as pieces from the collection would surely boost their business. Carmen promised that they would be represented at the auction and thanked the ladies for the personal invitation.

With the key suspects invited, they had one last stop on their way back to Lubrín, and that was to check in on the printer, who also doubled as the webpage designer for the event. Camilla had also plugged the event into the local newspaper, radio, and television advertising slots. By the time they met with Andie that evening for their usual feedback session, the town was already abuzz with the news of the auction.

The days flew by rapidly, and before they knew it, the moment had arrived. Of course, Camilla was truly a force to be reckoned with. She was like a tornado, volcano, and tsunami all rolled into one. And under her efficient stewardship, they were almost all set. She had insisted that they wear designer evening gowns as an absolute, non-negotiable point of order, and Kelly wouldn't dare cross Camilla when she was on this kind of organisational trajectory.

The conference hall had been transformed into a glamorous, world-class venue with elegant drapery and decorative Spanish columns. Water features created a soft and soothing accompaniment to the live eight-piece orchestra. A red carpet extended from the foyer all the way down the centre aisle of the hall itself, effectively separating the floor into two. Each guest received a welcome drink and pack containing a brochure, a numbered bid sign that correlated with the guest's registration number, a little chocolate, and an authentic replica of Paula de Eguiluz on a sterling silver keychain as a memento from the event. Kelly added that as a tribute to her ancestral legacy. And she knew it would rile those who hated Paula and believed her to have been a witch.

Kelly had to take a few doses of the herbal calming drops she always needed in these kinds of situations before allowing Camilla to drag her off to the foyer. Kelly's evening gown made her feel like she was playing Evita Perón, except Kelly knew that she was no Madonna. Her heels were already killing her. She just wanted to flee to the sanctuary of the holding room where her comfy bedroom slippers were waiting for her, but the first guests had already arrived. Oh well. There's no escape for me now, she thought with resignation.

"Surprise!" shrieked Camilla as she whirled Kelly to the entrance, where a dashing and devilishly handsome Dimitri Vázquez stood waiting for her. A shy smile danced on his face as he said, "Good evening, Kelly. Camilla thought it would be a good idea if you had someone standing by your side while you greeted the guests. You know, as a translator?" He was clearly nervous, as he was rambling a little.

"That was a great idea. Thank you, Camilla. But you are still recovering from..." she trailed off, raising her fingers to his temple where his stitches were still visible despite Camilla's cover-up job with concealer and powder.

"I am so sorry for the danger I had placed you in, Dimitri. I – can you ever forgive me?" implored Kelly, still gutted.

"There is nothing to forgive. Would I be here if I blamed you for what happened? And what kind of friend would I be if I had? Let's just try to enjoy the evening and give them all something to chat about for years to come, shall we, señorita?" he asked, giving her his arm – his smile was a rather charming weapon when he chose to use it.

Together, Kelly and Dimitri made an elegant and warm welcoming committee, and the guests entering the venue were in high spirits. Kelly was grateful to Camilla for her thoughtfulness, as mischievous and sneaky as she was. Dimitri was wonderful with the guests. The female guests of all ages especially took readily to him, finding his shy, scholarly manner appealing.

Ushers, some of whom were strategically placed undercover cops and friends of Andie's, showed the guests to their seats. Kelly was pleased that all four of their prime suspects had shown up. This is going to work! she thought optimistically. The culprits will be unveiled tonight. I am sure of it.

Each guest was greeted with a flute of champagne, which Kelly handed out with a smile that eventually hurt her face as much as her heels pinched her toes and made her arches ache. Still, it would all be worth it in the end when the police arrested the ringleader of the artefact robberies – and, possibly, Aunt Judy's murderer.

With their champagne in hand, guests were then directed to the registration table to sign in and collect their packs before entering the hall, where the ushers showed them to their seats. Dinner was served at 7:00 p.m. sharp. The starter was an interesting combination of chicken croquetas with a uniquely piquant citrus-infused dipping sauce, gambas al ajillo or garlic shrimp (no respectable Almerían dinner would be complete without it), and a delicious serving of tortilla española with a smoked paprika and chorizo twist. From what Kelly observed, the guests were already impressed with the menu. There was a steady flow of sangria to wet the palate and quench the thirst.

Kelly and Camilla unobtrusively walked around to ensure that the guests were happy and to add that personal touch. During the meal, a few entertaining dances and musical items kept the guests in good spirits while they ate.

The main course consisted of several gourmet dishes. Pisto, Spanish garlic mushrooms and octopus in tomato sauce accompanied bacon-wrapped stuffed dates and sweet potato pockets filled with chorizo, crunchy peppers, and sour cream. Other treats included smoked paprika chicken with toasted hazelnut picada, salmon with lemon roasted rice, and a scrumptious Spanish pork with orange and poppyseed salad to go with it all. By the end of the main course, the guests were in great spirits, and there was absolutely no tension in the hall. Of course, Camilla devoted a copious amount of attention to the Duque, who seemed to have a perpetually displeased look on his face. He hardly drank anything and only picked at his food without appetite. Kelly recalled his grand entrance to the auction and was never more glad to have had Dimitri by her side at that moment.

A sleek black Rolls Royce had pulled up to the red carpet, and out stepped the Duque Carlos Miguel Luis XI. Despite having left middle age, he did sport a rather impressive physique beneath his perfectly tailored dark tuxedo, which he wore with a detailed and gold embellished waistcoat. The traditional blue sash was fastened over his waistcoat, and a silk stock and paisley satin dressage riding stock bib with an elaborate gold stock pin with cufflinks to match completed the Duque's outfit. Stepping into the foyer in his black brogues of the highest quality as if it were his coronation as king, the Duque towered over Kelly in what she felt was a leer, while his eyes bored into her very soul with their icy stare. "So, this is the heir of Paula de Eguiluz, hey?" He scanned her thoroughly for several heart-stopping moments before asking with a sneer, "We hope that you haven't reproduced?"

"No – no, Your Grace. Not yet," replied Kelly.

"Well, I suppose we must be grateful for small mercies." His voice was thick with condescension. Thankfully, Camilla trotted toward them, ably rescuing Kelly from the Duque's steely gaze. Kelly grabbed Dimitri's arm for support the moment Camilla ushered the Duque away.

"What the hell was that?" gasped Kelly, her breath ragged from the encounter.

Dimitri patted her chilly hand in comfort and simply said, "Royals; they sure can be a pain in the posterior." And they shared a much-needed chuckle.

Luckily, the prospect of dessert lightened Kelly's mood and removed the bitter taste of that cold interaction with the Duque. Dessert was a choice between a decadent turrón pavlova and a serving of leche frita served with syrupy fruit and a shot of drinking chocolate. Guests were at liberty to select which they preferred while the most famous Spanish opera singer they could book at such short notice, serenaded them with an uplifting aria, which left the guests in silent wonder.

After a full hour and a half of gorging themselves on the decadent Spanish fare, it was finally time to move on to the main event of the evening: the auction.

16

Terror Trip

Kelly was never more grateful than she was now to be safely back behind the scenes in her comfy bedroom slippers. She threw a shawl over her evening gown so as to not get any stains on it and tucked into the beautifully packed takeaway dinner that Camilla had thoughtfully arranged to be sent to her.

She would have liked to have had Dimitri keep her company, but Isabella had latched onto him at some point, insisted that he be seated next to her, and then proceeded to talk his ear off about her organisation and its efforts. In all fairness, Dimitri seemed to be enthralled by the discussion too. It was a great opportunity for him to network with other historians and collectors, and Kelly didn't want to be selfish and monopolise his attention. Besides, he'd been such a huge help with everything. She was delighted that he had made it to the auction. Furthermore, she knew that she was safe since Andie had Gustavo Costa follow her at a discreet distance. She was certain that he was just outside like a sentinel, keeping her safe.

To get the auction started, a short video clip about the life and times of Paula de Eguiluz played from a projector. *I wonder how the members of the 'Tree Gang' and their sympathisers are able to stomach this video,* thought Kelly in amusement. The video was then followed by a reel containing details about each piece to be auctioned that evening, excluding Paula's journal. That would be the showstopper and a complete surprise. Kelly groaned at the idea of putting those mile-high shoes back on and marching out there with the journal at the end. But she had a long wait before that happened, and she knew that Camilla would bustle in before then to touch up her makeup and ensure that she looked perfect before she had to go out there to face those upper-class, uptight types.

So Kelly happily chomped on her dinner, enjoying the solace of finally getting a respite from the spotlight, even if it would be short-lived. She had never tasted anything quite so flavourful as the bacon-wrapped stuffed dates, and she immediately decided that it was her new, all-time favourite food in the world.

While she ate, Kelly listened to the auction over the speakers in the anterooms, but the whole event was conducted in Spanish, so she didn't understand most of it. While Kelly valued her Aunt Judy's memory, she was not all that interested in material things, favouring experiences more. Admittedly, auctioning off the collection did evoke a twinge of guilt, mainly because Aunt Judy had spent years safeguarding it, but Kelly did not wish to be tied down to the ghost of Paula or the ludicrous prophecy and the lore surrounding it.

It sounded like the auction was going very well, indeed, and she knew that Camilla would be making her appearance – makeup kit at the ready – to touch up Kelly's face as if she were one of the items up for auction herself. So, she didn't look up when she heard someone enter the room, even though she was facing away from the door.

"I knew you would be coming—" But Kelly did not get to finish her sentence, as a strong arm held her firmly in place while a chemical-soaked cloth was clapped over her nose and mouth.

Stumbling forward, Kelly tried to remember a self-defence move or two she'd learnt a few years back, but all she managed to do was infuriate her unseen assailant even further. Her heartbeat grew erratic and then started to slow down. Her vision blurred as she flailed her arms, tearing at the forearms of her attacker. The last thing she heard was the sound of something small fall to the floor before she did.

By the time she came to, Kelly felt nauseous, and her head hurt fiercely. She had been gagged, bound, and thrown into the boot of a vehicle. However, the car was stationary. As Kelly became fully conscious, she realised that her assailant might have slipped back into the auction unnoticed. Presently, the sounds of sirens blaring toward her filled her with hope.

Perfect timing. The cops will find me, thought Kelly optimistically, as she tried to draw attention to her location. But she found herself unable to move and the gag remained painfully secure about her mouth. She could hear all the commotion outside and wore herself out futilely, trying to make some sort of noise, until she lay quite spent in the confines of the trunk – her presence undetected despite the strong police presence all around her. She was invisible.

Kelly found herself gripped by the most overwhelming sense of terror she had ever experienced in her life. The cold sweat that dripped down her spine made her shudder involuntarily as it dawned on her that she was now at the mercy of these criminals who had been circling like a flock of ravenous vultures, waiting for the perfect opportunity to strike. *And we gave it to them on a silver platter!* thought Kelly, bitterly. *How could I have been so stupid to not have seen this coming? So much for our strategy,* she berated herself. *I was nowhere near the panic button! I should have been more alert. We expected them to strike once they knew we had the journal. That was going to be our trump card. What do they want with me?*

After what seemed like days, but in reality was probably a couple of hours at the most, the car finally started to move – slowly at first, but after a few minutes, it seemed like they were speeding on winding roads that sometimes felt like a steep climb, and in other places, it felt like they were careening down a valley at breakneck speed. Pretty soon, Kelly could not tell up from down and her head swam painfully while her tummy lurched uncomfortably as the driver continued recklessly.

After a long, circuitous terror trip, the car finally stopped. The boot opened and a burly man with a severely scarred face threw a bag over Kelly's head so she would not be able to see where she was. He then carried her up a short flight of stairs and into a building. Kelly sensed they had moved from the crisp outdoors to a warm indoor space. *Could it be a house? It feels warm and cosy. Not what she expected.*

But her hopes were dashed when she was taken down several flights of stairs into what immediately felt cold and dank. Kelly thought that she was in a basement of some sort or a cave room, and the mustiness of the air assaulted her nostrils as her chest heaved, trying to find oxygen in the fetid air.

Kelly was unceremoniously plonked onto a chair, where her restraints were adjusted so that her arms were wrapped uncomfortably around the chair and fastened at the back. Brisk footsteps on the stairs echoed and then stopped in front of her. A familiar cologne teased her nostrils. *Where have I smelled this fragrance before?* She wracked her brain but could not place the scent, except she knew that it was familiar to her.

Meanwhile, Camilla realised that she would have to check in on Kelly, and, grabbing her makeup kit, dashed off to the holding rooms where Kelly had prepared a little sanctuary for herself in advance. As Camilla approached the door, however, she was aghast at the sight of Gustavo Costa lying sprawled out on the floor. He was dead!

A throwaway container of food had crashed to the ground. Clearly, he had been poisoned. Camilla had forgotten to arrange for Gustavo to receive a dinner pack. Whoever did this must have prepared a poisoned pack and given it to him.

Frantic now, Camilla flung open the door to where Kelly was supposed to be sitting – she was gone! "No, no, no, no, no, noooo!" Camilla's pulse began to race, and she remained rooted to the floor, in the grip of a full-on anxiety attack. Her airways became constricted, and she began to gasp for air, hyperventilating as a cold sweat enveloped her. *Kelly! They've taken Kelly,* she repeated to herself.

Finally, scrambling for Kelly's evening bag, Camilla fumbled to find the panic button and depressed it. Within the space of a minute, Andie and two of the 'ushers' were at her side. Andie recognised that Camilla was coming out of a panic attack and could not speak as yet. "Hold on, Camilla. Help is on its way," asserted Andie, calmly looking into Camilla's dazed eyes.

Then, taking her gently but firmly by the shoulders, Andie spoke slowly and deliberately, "Camilla, I'm going to need you to calm down and tell me everything you saw, okay?"

Camilla managed a rapid nod and, gulping down her anxiety, said in a shaky voice, "I came to the back to... to touch up Kelly's makeup since she would be carrying in the showstopper. Then... then..." She trailed off, remembering the sight of Gustavo Costa lying face down with the food strewn in front of him, and the nausea threatened to overtake her.

"Stay with me now, Camilla. This is important. Go on," coaxed Andie, as patiently as she could muster.

"I saw Gustavo lying there. And I knew something was terribly wrong. So, I rushed in to find that Kelly was gone. The dinner pack that I personally put together for her was only half-eaten." Camilla burst into helpless tears.

"Did you also give Gustavo his meal pack, Camilla?" asked Andie, trying to understand.

"N-no. I had clean forgotten about him. Someone else gave him the packed dinner, and I'll bet it was poisoned!"

"Thanks, Camilla. My people are on it. We will find her, I promise," vowed Andie solemnly.

"Cordon off all entrances and exits discreetly. Let the auction play itself out. None of the guests knew about the showstopper. We will leave it out of the programme. No one is to know that anything is amiss," instructed Andie into her slim walkie-talkie.

"Ramírez and Gómez, come with me. We need to account for all the guests. Inform me if anyone is missing. *Vámonos!*" Andie left hurriedly toward the hall while others checked the parking area and discreetly questioned the valet personnel.

Camilla sat dejectedly in the same seat Kelly had set up for herself. While she was staring at the floor, trying to come to terms with what was happening, her eyes were drawn to something glittering on the floor. Reaching to the floor, Camilla found a rather exquisitely designed cufflink. She was about to pick it up when she realised that there might be a print on it that the authorities could use to track down Kelly's kidnapper. So she called Andie back.

"Great work, Camilla," Andie said with a smile. "We will run this for prints," she said, taking pictures of the cufflink, which she had placed into a clear evidence bag.

"What is going on here?" asked Dimitri.

He had finally managed to extricate himself from Isabella's clutches and came to check on Kelly. "Where's Kelly?" he asked, expectantly.

"She's been kidnapped, Dimitri," Andie informed him worriedly.

"All the guests are accounted for. A few had left to go to the bathroom or take a phone call. But they returned to the hall within ten minutes." Andie updated them on developments, as the more eyes and ears they had looking for clues, the more likely were their chances. But at that moment, things did not look promising.

"What do you have there, Andie?" asked Dimitri, gesturing to the cufflink.

"It is a cufflink that may or may not belong to the kidnapper," explained Andie, and then, speaking into her walkie-talkie once again, said, "Team, check the cuffs of every male guest as they leave. Our suspect is missing a cufflink."

"This cufflink looks familiar, actually," muttered Dimitri, trying to remember where he had seen it before. But he just could not place it.

Dimitri tried to remember all the male guests he had welcomed, but too much had happened this evening for him to think clearly. "Andie, could you help me get access to the footage from the camera in the foyer, please?" pleaded Dimitri. "It might help me remember." For his ears only he added: "I have got to help them find Kelly before it is too late."

Andie arranged for Dimitri to have full access to the camera footage.

"We will run the cufflink through our database as well," explained Andie. "We will track them down, Dimitri. But if you come across anything on those tapes that might help us, give me a call." She gave his arm a reassuring squeeze before rushing off to check on the guards at the gate.

"Nobody left the auction as yet, ma'am," confirmed the guard. "You can confirm it from the video footage in the control room. But I've been here all night and – nothing."

The auction concluded and, without authorisation, Andie and her team were unable to search the cars as they exited the parking area. But they did set up a police roadblock along the main road leading out of the area. Unfortunately, there were numerous little roads and pathways that the kidnappers could have used to make their getaway.

Although she hated to admit it, Andie seemed to have come to a dead end. Their only hope was the single cufflink Camilla found on the floor of the holding area.

About fifteen minutes after the last guest had left, Dimitri came sprinting down to the holding area, where Andie was doing a last sweep of the place, trying to find more clues.

"I've got it. I remember where I had seen the cufflinks. And I went back to the video footage from the cameras in the foyer. It belongs to the Duque! He came in wearing them, and he had no cufflinks on when he left!" cried Dimitri triumphantly.

"Are you certain, Dimitri?" asked Andie, not wanting to ruffle any aristocratic feathers with false accusations.

"Yes. I am sure," confirmed Dimitri. Then he proceeded to show Andie the camera footage.

"Alright, team, gather all the intel you can on the Duque, his whereabouts, and movements. Get Tech to pinpoint his location via his cell phone, stat!"

"On it, boss," affirmed one of the plainclothes officers.

"We will find her," she asserted, more to herself than Dimitri.

17

Unveiling and Surveilling

He sat there watching her. It felt surreal that they had found her after a lifetime of dedication to the moment of victory that was surely imminent. He thought back to his initiation at the tender age of twelve. His father was exceedingly proud of how well he had done in his trial in the Guerrero Arena where he had competed with five other youths in a battle of wits, strength, and agility in preparation for their future roles in the *Cazadores de la Bruja Poderosa* – or 'Hunters of the Mighty Witch'.

It was a curious cult that reminded him of a bedtime story his *mami* would tell him about the troll who would protect, feed, and fatten the children he captured to then enjoy a great, succulent feast of them when he was truly famished. And his *papi* had told him numerous times, "*Mijo,* like a good farmer, we protect the young grapes on their vines even though they taste sour; then we wait and wait patiently until they are ready and at their sweetest before crushing them to make our wine, giving liquid courage to he who drinks it in victory."

He was now a mature man of sixty-four. Finally, the grapes were ready after hundreds of years of protection, patience, and perseverance. And he could not wait to taste the wine that had taken this long to reach maturity. He felt the privilege that he had lived to see this moment when others, more dedicated than he had been, had been claimed by Time.

Kelly drifted in and out of consciousness. They had drugged her with an injection, and her brain moved intermittently from a state of wakeful fogginess to being out cold. At some point, she must have fallen asleep because, when she came to, it was already the next morning, judging from the sounds and activities around her. The sack covering her head was light and porous enough for her to see that night had become day, but little else.

Kelly still had no idea where she was or who her captors were. She'd heard male voices speaking mockingly in Spanish very close to her face. They seemed to be taunting her. *Do these clowns not know that I don't understand Spanish? Or maybe they don't really care if I understand them or not,* she thought. By now, Kelly was both terrified and exhausted. She kept hearing the word *bruja* which she knew meant 'witch' in Spanish. *I must be at the HQ of the 'Tree Gang!'* determined Kelly, her fear mingled with excitement. Her plan had worked – just not in the way she had imagined. They did manage to flush out the gang. *I know that Andie will find me. I did rip off some item of jewellery from the kidnapper. I heard it fall to the ground. Andie will find it and somehow track me down.*

"But why are you keeping our important guest locked here in the storeroom? And on Saint Valentine's Day, too," came a familiar male voice. There was that distinct cologne again.

"Get that thing off her head at once!" He spoke in English for her benefit and then repeated the instruction in Spanish.

Kelly felt like her eyeballs were being skewered by a hot rod. They had switched on a bright white fluorescent light that hurt her eyes and she struggled to focus. The henchman closest to her also removed her gag as her eyes adjusted. And then, shocked recognition set in.

"It is *you*!" she spewed in disgust.

"I'm afraid so, *bruja* – I mean, Señorita Simpson," mocked the Duque, his eyes dancing in amusement at Kelly's pathetic plight.

"I must apologise for my men's rough treatment of you. You see, they don't particularly like witches very much. And your family has a special place of importance on the list of people they hate. It is indeed unfortunate," explained the Duque, as if they were long-time friends.

"Kindly show our guest to her living quarters. *¡Ándale!*"

"You can refresh yourself, and I have arranged for a more comfortable change of clothes for you as well. We shall talk after that," said the Duque amiably, as though Kelly really was his guest and he the gracious host.

"I am *not* your guest! Let me go immediately, Duque, or you will regret it!" Kelly tried to shout, but her voice was hoarse, and it sounded more like a strangled squeak.

Her whole body felt like lead, and she was severely dehydrated. Kelly was taken to another room, where her arms and legs were unbound. It seemed like they were in a small house or business premises in a remote region. All the windows were sealed, guarded, and shuttered. The room was more like a narrow cell with a bathroom. A fresh set of clothes and a towel lay on the single bed. The bathroom was a tiny space with a toilet and shower, for which Kelly was grateful, as she was in desperate need of both. The spout let out a trickle of tepid water, but at least the soap looked like it was an upmarket homemade beauty bar. It was marvellously fragrant, and it lathered beautifully.

Unfortunately, there was no shampoo, so Kelly had to tie her hair up into a knot.

I know exactly why he has me here. In fact, I figured they'd do something like this. But I did not think it was the Duque. I really pegged Mateo Hernández as the culprit. He had been so mysterious and evasive about his business. Kelly let her thoughts run wild while she got dressed.

It is surprising that he hadn't ordered a lab coat as well, thought Kelly wryly. She knew that the Duque believed the prophecy, and he knew that she was the last female descendent of Paula de Eguiluz. In fact, she recalled that he had confirmed that when he arrived at the auction.

Presently, the same henchman burst into the room. Fortunately, Kelly had just pulled the white T-shirt down over her breasts, and he only caught a glimpse of her belly. "Pervert! Don't you knock?" spat Kelly. This simply amused him and he laughed heartily.

"Come," he said, and grabbed her arm roughly.

She was taken to an ancient kitchen. It was kept very clean, but everything in it was at least fifty years old. The Duque sat waiting for her at the little table with a plastic tablecloth with different kinds of peppers printed all over it.

"Ah, Kelly Simpson. Do sit down and have something to eat. You have been unconscious for almost an entire day. You must be famished," said the Duque, again acting as though she were a guest in his home. But this could not be the Duque's home – it must be the headquarters for the gang. Kelly knew she had to keep up her strength and, even though she had lost her appetite, forced herself to eat. *This food isn't half bad, actually,* thought Kelly, pleasantly surprised. She was only allowed a plastic fork. The Duque watched her eat. It was quite unnerving. "I like a woman with a robust appetite. *Bravo*!"

Kelly knew that she should be scared out of her wits, but she felt surprisingly calm. "Not that I am not enjoying this great little visit in your country palace, Your Grace. But why have you brought me here?" asked Kelly, smiling sweetly.

"I am not sure how much you know, Señorita Simpson, but you are the descendent of a witch who wielded great power and magic. Don't be fooled by other, more sedate historical accounts. Have you heard of the Prophecy of Paula de Eguiluz?" he probed. His beady black eyes bore into hers while his bushy eyebrows looked like wriggly caterpillars chasing each other across the furrowed dunes of his domed forehead. Kelly smothered a giggle – *Am I high or something? It must be the effects of whatever it is they've been injecting into me.*

"I did hear something about it, but I think that maybe a lot got lost in translation. What do you know about it, Your Grace?" asked Kelly, trying to mimic his tone of normality – she was just a guest, enjoying the Duque's hospitality after all – nothing amiss with that.

"According to the legend, Paula de Eguiluz had passed down her powers to her daughter, who, in turn, passed it down to her daughter, and her daughter. Over the generations, these powers may have manifested in overt ways or they may have remained dormant. In many instances, a daughter of Paula de Eguiluz did not even know what power she had inherited."

"Pretty much like diabetes and cardiac disease?" mocked Kelly, with a snigger.

"That is just the truth serum talking. One of the side effects is a warped sense of humour. I am not offended. It just means that the serum is taking effect. Good." The Duque seemed unperturbed.

"Truth – what now?" slurred Kelly.

"Anyway, as I was saying," he continued. "The prophecy states that the very last daughter of Paula de Eguiluz would have the power to create a potion that would grant the one who consumes it unlimited power, wealth, and longevity. The only proviso is that the end of Paula's line must be allowed to be reached completely naturally. If there is any interference in the progression of the ancestral line, the prophecy will not be fulfilled," explained the Duque, animatedly.

"Ah..." began Kelly with a knowing grin. "So don't you think that whoever made up this prophecy business – and I have a fairly good idea that it may have been Paula herself – wanted to safeguard her lineage? I mean, what better way to ensure that her children survived? She wasn't a witch. She was a genius!" Kelly had a severe case of the giggles. But the Duque continued, unruffled.

"In addition, Paula had imbued some of her most treasured artefacts from her extensive collection with her powers. According to the prophecy, when the last daughter makes the potion, the one who consumes it must be surrounded by as many of Paula's valuables as possible because it will act as a catalyst, magnifying the potency of the potion and whatever spell that goes with it." By then, the Duque had talked himself into a frenzy of excitement, and concluded by saying, "And here you are – the last daughter of Paula de Eguiluz. Oh, how long we have served to protect you and your ancestors. It was just unfortunate about your Aunt Judy," said the Duque apologetically.

"So you did murder her!" accused Kelly in disgust and grief.

"It was not ideal, I know. But unavoidable. We knew that even though Judy remained childless, her sister had a daughter. But we could not track you down. And Judy would not co-operate with us. Since we knew that Paula's succession was from Judy's sister and not Judy herself..." He shrugged.

"Aunt Judy was expendable," realised Kelly, heartbroken and livid at the same time. His silence, an admission of guilt.

"I am sorry about the loss of your aunt. But it was a breakthrough for us," he continued without mercy. "Because it brought you here. At last, after years of searching, we finally found you, Kelly Simpson. And you are just over the age of thirty-five – exactly like the prophecy foretold," he exclaimed gleefully.

"I could still have children, Duque. This is the twenty-first century. Women have healthy children well into their forties now," retaliated Kelly, weakly. But her heart mourned her beloved mother-figure, Judy Fargo, all over again.

"I know that you are still mourning your aunt, but I need you to make that potion before you disappear back under the rock from whence you came, young lady. And from the sound of your accent, it may be a provincial town in England. Am I right?"

"Listen, Your Grace. I understand that you have spent your whole life trying to track down Paula's daughters and that this whole potion-prophecy-legend thing means everything to you. But you have taken someone who has meant the world to me. And I am afraid that you are just going to have to kill me like you killed my Aunt Judy. Because I am not mixing any damn potion for the likes of you, not even a cup of tea! You got that, Dukie?" By this time, Kelly's voice had built to a crescendo, and her face had turned quite purple.

"Oh dear. I can see that I have upset you. *Lo siento,*" he apologised, reaching out to wipe Kelly's cheek. But one threatening look from her stopped his hand in mid-air.

"Felipe," he commanded, clicking his fingers. And the henchman named Felipe promptly grabbed Kelly's arms and dragged her back to her room, locking the door behind him.

"Let me out of here!" she screamed uselessly, banging on the door until her hands hurt.

"I've called the Duque's residence on the pretext of discussing an auction emergency, trying to get a hold of anyone who may still be awake. But the night guard said that Duque Carlos had left the auction and gone straight to one of his other estates for the weekend and would be indisposed until Tuesday or Wednesday next week," announced Camilla mournfully.

"Alright, but we will go to the estate and check for ourselves how many people are on the Duque's property at this time of the night," decided Andie. "We've got specialist surveillance equipment and other options that we'll use for that." It was two in the morning and the property would be on a skeleton staff if the Duque was going to be away.

"I just realised that it is Valentine's Day, and our Kelly's life is in such grave danger," cried Camilla. Her bottom lip trembled, and fresh tears rolled down her cheeks. Kelly was like a little sister to her, and she felt responsible for not protecting her from those thugs.

"We will get her back, Camilla. Don't lose hope. She will be alright," comforted Andie.

"I am coming with you to save her." Dimitri emerged from the kitchen with coffee for everyone. They had set up their base at Camilla's house.

"That's very brave of you, Dimitri. But we are dealing with very dangerous people here, and you would be more of a liability than help. I want you to please stay here under the watchful eyes of my plainclothes officers. Inspector Gamero has been brought up to speed, and he is sending me his best people," lied Andie.

She did not trust anyone at that point, not even the local police. If she needed any more help, she would use operatives she had worked with in the past, people she knew she could count on. Andie had already brought in Fitzgerald and Jones, who had retired and gone into partnership as a private investigative operation in Granada. They had come to Almería on the day of the auction to provide support if Andie required it. Andie made the call, and the three of them met on the outskirts of Almería City.

"Thank you for the much-needed assist on this one, you two. I don't know who the Duque has in his pocket in this town, but you can bet that at least some of the higher-ups of the police force are sure to be on his payroll. So, we're going to have to go dark on this one. You still in?" Andie was respected for her 'no bullshit' policy. She believed that if you were going to ask someone to risk their life for you, you'd better be upfront with what they were getting themselves into.

"We're in, Spears. How many times have you saved our bacon in the field?" replied Jones with a nod.

"I'm in," affirmed Fitzgerald, a man of few words.

"Good. We will check the Duque's palace, but I don't think that he would be foolish enough to bring Kelly to his main residence. He has three other homes in Spain, but seeing as how he and his associates had bought most of the items on auction tonight, I'd say that our best bet is a property not too far from the auction venue. That would be the ranch he owns on the outskirts of Lubrín."

Andie briefed her little team on the best course of action. Within fifteen minutes, it had become clear that the Duque was not, in fact, at his palace in Almería City, and they swiftly proceeded to the ranch. The place was much too heavily guarded for a simple ranch. Granted, the land itself was expansive and there seemed to be several buildings on the property. They counted seven in total from the reconnaissance drone they sent up. From heat signatures, it looked like there were six guards walking the perimeter with two guard dogs on leashes.

"Well, we sure have our work cut out for us, gentlemen," whispered Andie as they gathered intel on the place. Using the surveillance gadgets, they picked up on some activity in the little dilapidated house at the far end of the property, but they would have to get closer to get a better idea of how many people were in there. It was curious that they were awake at this hour. "Let's zero in on that building. I want as much intel as we can get without drawing any attention to ourselves. Jones, you're our eyes and ears. Fitz and I will cover the perimeter. The sun will be up in a little while, and we will have to wait for the cover of night once more to complete the mission. Set your watches. We will meet you at your perch in thirty minutes, Jones," instructed Andie as they passed black face paint around – it was part of their camouflage attire. They synced chronometers and split up.

Jones, who was the youngest and most agile of the team, climbed up the tallest tree closest to the electric fence at the far edge of the ranch – near the targeted building. The detection equipment picked up another five people in that building alone: one seated in the centre of the ground floor with a guard standing watch, while two others were stationed outside. Upstairs, another individual was seated at a table, drinking coffee or another hot beverage. The seated individual on the ground floor seemed to be unconscious, their head lolling uncomfortably to one side. "That is Kelly," Jones whispered. "I am sure of it!"

They remained hidden until morning so that they could observe the Duque's movements and operations. Team K – 'K' for Kelly – took shifts so that each of them got at least two hours of shut-eye at a time. They confirmed that the Duque was on the property, as he had moved from the old building they had dubbed Target A to another, more comfortable-looking building at 9:15 a.m. The guards had changed shifts promptly at 7:00 a.m. with the focus being on Target A.

Kelly had been moved twice. From the first location to another room where she had a shower, and then she was taken to the kitchen where she was given a meal while another person sat across from her – possibly the Duque. She seemed to be unharmed and mobile, which meant that it would be easier to extract her when the time came.

Team K worked out an extraction plan and continued to observe undetected.

18

Do or Die

"Kelly is a tough, resourceful girl, Dimitri. She will find a way to stay alive until Andie finds her."

"*Sí,* but I just hate that I have to just sit here and do nothing. I want to help get her out of that madman's clutches, Señorita López," complained Dimitri in frustration.

"You really care about Kelly, don't you?" asked Camilla knowingly. She was trying to calm him down.

"*Sí,* very much. But what will she think of me, hiding in here when I should be out there doing everything I can to rescue her or die trying?" He sat down with his head in his hands.

"I have known Andie for a long, long time, Dimitri. She will get Kelly out of there and those thugs will be brought to justice, mark my words."

Kelly tried to remember the ingredients and method for the Elixir of Life recipe. But she was too nervous to get it right. The kitchen had been converted into a makeshift apothecary but she remained trapped in the little bedroom.

After what felt like days but, in reality, may have been two to three hours, Kelly was brought to the kitchen where the Duque sat expectantly. He had been reverentially paging through Paula's journal. Kelly was livid but tried to keep calm and at least maintain a cool-headed facade while inwardly, she was like a volcano ready to erupt.

Kelly pieced together what must have happened. *He must have stolen the journal when he kidnapped me. It had been lying in place on a display stand on the table next to me, ready to be brought out for the finale.*

But where was Gustavo Costa? Why didn't he stop the Duque in his tracks?

"I had spent most of my adult life searching for this journal," admitted Duque Carlos Miguel Luis XI, with an air of solemnity and awe. "And you were going to auction it to the highest bidder? How dare you?" he exploded with anger, and his voice thundered across the room. But instead of quaking in her slippers, Kelly had become strangely quiet and resolved.

"In case you didn't get the memo, Dukie, that journal belongs to me. Have you forgotten who I am?" she asked, trying to adopt a regal tone.

"I am sorry, Señorita Simpson." He instantly calmed down. "It was a momentary lapse. You clearly do not have the same kind of reverence for the effects of Paula de Eguiluz that we do." He took a deep breath and then spoke in a much more amiable tone.

"Now, I am going to need you to make the Elixir of Life for me right now. I have sourced most of the ingredients according to the recipe. The rest of them should arrive by this afternoon. While you were resting, we made a translation of the recipe for you to work with. Study it carefully because one wrong move, and we could be destroyed. In the meantime, my men will carefully prepare the room for my transformation."

Transformation? Who does he think he is? Optimus Prime in the old barn or something? thought Kelly, trying to keep her spirits up.

The place was crawling with the Duque's men as they worked intensively on preparing the room. There was a steady stream of them carefully bringing in artefacts from Paula's collection, amassed by all necessary means.

Kelly grudgingly admitted, "That is quite a collection you have there, Dukie. I suppose there are no prizes for guessing who was behind all the artefact robberies." The Duque was silent. Perhaps her words were getting to him. So she pressed on.

"*Tsk, tsk*, Dukie. Look how far we have stooped – murder and larceny. And now, kidnapping. I have never come across a royal who is also a career criminal! Shame on you," she rebuked.

"You will not take such an arrogant tone with me once I come fully into my own powers, *bruja.* Then, you will be begging me to let you into my organisation as we slowly take over Spain, Europe, and eventually, the whole world!"

He really believes this stuff! Boy, that Paula was a really convincing woman. No wonder she eluded the Spanish Inquisition twice! Gosh, I hope that I can elude these goons just this once. Where are you, Andie? she thought to herself, getting a bit worked up at the sight of all the foot traffic past the kitchen where she sat with the Duque, pretending to study the recipe and match it to the ingredients they had already brought her.

"Er, Dukie. I have noticed that the key ingredient, *Taxus baccata,* is missing. I can't make the elixir without it, even with my witchy superpowers," she announced arrogantly.

"Not to worry, little diva. It is on its way," he crooned.

"And are all these goons going to be here while I work? I mean, I can't concentrate with a herd of elephants stampeding up and down here, you know!" She was trying to mimic movie stars who made demands on their producers, threatening to not perform unless their demands were met.

The Duque took a deep breath to calm himself but ignored her last remarks.

Presently, a scholarly-looking man of around Kelly's age came in meekly carrying a shopping bag made of cloth.

"Ah, finally!" cheered the Duque, clapping the newcomer on the back and then hugging him.

"Señorita Kelly Simpson, last daughter of Paula de Eguiluz, meet my brilliant nephew, Teodoro Miguel. He is a genius and has been studying everything about witchcraft, chemistry, and herbalism to be able to help you. You are *destined* to work together, no?"

"It is a pleasure to meet you, at last, Señorita Simpson. I have been hoping that this day would come when I could be of some little assistance to you," he said shyly.

Boy! This guy is even more pathetic than I am! He definitely does not get out much.

"Thank you. I wish I could say that I am pleased to meet you. You know, for people who claim to be in awe of me, you sure have a funny way of showing it," whined Kelly, trying to gauge how far she could play the diva with the new guy.

"Actually," he began, pushing his glasses up to the bridge of his nose. Kelly fantasised about breaking the glasses – until she realised that without them he would look like Voldemort. "Did you know that in some ancient cultures, it is customary to treat sacrificial animals with the utmost respect and reverence, feeding them well and showing them loads of love and consideration before they are sacrificed?"

Oh, boy! He is an insufferable know-it-all! thought Kelly, rolling her eyes.

"So, what you're saying is that this event is going to end with me being a sacrificial lamb? Is that what you're saying, Teo?" asked Kelly, getting up close to Teodoro in a threatening manner.

The Duque laughed appreciatively, clapping his hands. "I see that you two are going to get along like a house on fire! We will leave the two of you to work in peace now. You should have everything you need to make the potion. But if there is anything else you need, Teo, call for Felipe. *Señorita,* I wish you all the best. I know that you are a very powerful witch and will do a great job!"

"Yeah! Just call me Hermione Granger," mocked Kelly, looking witheringly at Teo, who recoiled as if she had turned him into a toad. *He is afraid of me. Wonderful! I can use that.*

"Oh, Dukie. I see that there isn't a shred of white and dark sage in here," said Kelly, in full diva mode.

"Yes, well, the recipe does not call for it..." blathered the Duque, looking at Teo for support.

"Well, any witch or wizard worth their saltpetre knows that before commencing work on a potion, all the energies in the area must be well-balanced by burning the highest grade of white and black sage in equal quantities in the vicinity," complained Kelly. All that extra research was paying off.

"I mean, if you're going to kidnap me, hold me captive and force me to make a potion, the least you can do is give a witch the proper ingredients to work with!" She threw her hands up in exasperation, really getting into her role now.

Of course, Teo immediately flipped open his laptop and confirmed, "She is right, *Tìo. Lo siento.*" He read from his screen: "It is advisable to cleanse the environment and balance all light and dark energies before embarking on any form of spell casting. This may be done by burning equal quantities of white and dark sage sticks and allowing the smoke to reach every corner of the space."

The Duque laid into his nephew in Spanish before going out to speak to Felipe, who immediately rushed off in a black SUV, raising dust as he sped away. It was the first glimpse that Kelly got of the outside, and she tried to memorise the lay of the land in the hope that she would need it if she managed to escape.

Feeling pleased with herself for being able to delay the process a bit longer, she busied herself by pretending to prepare the ingredients while she was frantically searching for something to use as a weapon. The Duque was much too distracted by the delay to notice, and it was the perfect chance to pocket any weapon she could find.

The guards and goons had been redistributed after a rather haggard-looking goon brought the Duque a report. This gave Kelly hope that Andie was making some progress.

"I must say, *Señorita,* I thought that your new friends would have valued you a lot more. My contacts in the police department say that nobody has reported you missing as yet. Your loose friend with the long legs, Camilla, is in her flat entertaining your professor friend. They are drinking wine and watching movies together as if you didn't even exist!" taunted the Duque.

"The only person unaccounted for is your old friend, Andie Spears. But what can she do, really? I understand that she has had some background in law enforcement as she does work with that boy scout, Gamero, from time to time. But as you can see, she would be outnumbered if she tried anything. Besides, we are completely off the grid. It would take them a very long time to find us here in the first place. But we are armed to the teeth and our surveillance tech is state of the art. So, don't allow yourself to become distracted by any hopes that the cavalry will ride in on their white steeds and rescue you, *bruja*. As soon as Felipe brings the herbs, you will get started, *comprende*?" he threatened menacingly, grabbing Kelly by the hair to reinforce his point.

"Wow! Don't get your knickers in a twist, Dukie. I am actually curious about whether or not this potion thing is going to work. I am sure you must know that I don't believe in all this mumbo jumbo. Don't you know that you should not underestimate your adversaries, Dukie?"

"Nobody's coming to save you, *bruja*," whispered the Duque close to her face before letting go of her hair with a violent shove.

"Alright, Jonesy," began Andie, "you will slide underneath the pickup truck when it returns like you did in Tbilisi, remember? Once he is safely inside and the truck stops, Fitz, you will create a distraction at the main house. And I will use the element of surprise to shoot out and scale the fence like we did in Operation Safari, with the blanket from the trunk, remember?"

They both nodded and carefully moved into position as the sun began to set on their long day of surveillance. Within a few minutes, the headlights from the pickup could be seen coming down the dirt road. Jones had placed a log across the road some distance from the ranch, forcing Felipe to stop and remove it. After which Jones was suspended under the vehicle and driving into the compound. Felipe leapt out of the truck, leaving the keys in the ignition as he rushed over to Target A to deliver the sage bundles. No sooner had he handed it to Kelly than all hell broke loose at the main entrance.

There was a loud explosion as the gate was blown to smithereens, and the electric fence deactivated. The Duque shouted out instructions in Spanish to his goons and then to Teodoro before turning to Kelly. "Keep going if you want to live through this, *bruja!*" And then he left, locking them in. Obviously, there were extra guards stationed outside. They could hear the commotion as everyone got to their battle stations.

"You heard my uncle, *señorita.* Let's get started." Teodoro pointed a taser at her and gestured to the kitchen work surface, where all the ingredients and apparatuses were set up. Kelly, bolstered by the commotion, which could only mean one thing – Andie was around, and she brought reinforcements – went over to the row of aprons on the hooks. She selected the cleanest-looking one and fastened it around herself – it was a delaying tactic, but it paid off. As she leaned against the counter, she felt something in the pocket of the apron. "Do you have matches or a lighter to light up the sage?" she asked Teo in a businesslike tone.

While he was busy lighting the sage bundles for her, Kelly found a little knife, the kind used to slice vegetables, in the pocket of the apron. To her delight, she found, among the spices, some cayenne pepper. She threw a tablespoon of it into the pocket of the apron as a weapon of her own. *Maybe I am a witch, after all,* she thought in amusement. She ensured that the entire area was covered in smoke before making her move. Teo, in an effort to speed things up, also waved a bundle of sage around. Kelly moved toward him, billowing sage smoke everywhere, especially near his eyes.

In one fluid motion, she threw the pepper into his eyes, disarmed him, and tasered him until he was out cold. She quickly gathered the remaining aprons and used them to strap the still-unconscious Teodoro to a chair. The Duque burst into the kitchen at that moment to find Kelly holding the taser at Teo's throat. Several goons assembled behind the Duque, and Kelly realised that she was gravely outnumbered.

Nevertheless, she shouted in what she hoped was a threatening voice, "Take one more step and your precious genius nephew's brains will be toast, Dukie."

The Duque carefully edged forward, trying to sound calm. "Now, listen, *Señorita*—"

"No, you listen, Dukie. Ask your goons to put down their weapons and you, too."

After what felt like an eternity, the Duque nodded to his men, who threw down their weapons. At that exact moment, Andie and her two teammates appeared with automatic firearms at the ready.

"Well, it is about damn time. I was thinking that I would have to rescue myself here!" proclaimed Kelly, her knees almost giving way from the strain of putting up a brave front when, in reality, she was scared out of her wits.

"Well, it seems like you were doing just fine on your own there, Kelly girl. I am very proud of you," said Andie with a smile before turning to the others. "Alright, everyone, march yourself to the storeroom until the cavalry gets here." As Fitz locked the door, the sound of sirens could be heard in the distance.

While Andie and her team had their hands full getting the Duque and his henchmen into the storeroom, Teo had come to. He swiftly moved, swinging around the chair he was tied to, knocking Kelly to the ground and broke free from his makeshift bonds. He grabbed Kelly around her waist and neck as she writhed and tried to twist out of his grip. "Andie! Help!" she screamed.

Luckily, she still had the apron on and while Andie tried to talk him down, she carefully reached into the pocket and found the little knife.

Letting her hand fall back to her side, she continued to plead, "Teo, I know that you are not like your uncle. You are a good person. Do you really want to be the one who killed the daughter of Paula de Eguiluz?"

His body froze at the thought of doing such a thing, and that was the opening she needed. Kelly drove the knife deep into Teo's thigh and managed to break free while he cried out in anguish. Gamero's men finally arrived, taking over the crime scene, bagging every one of the Duque's men and the Duque himself.

Kelly fell to the ground, horrified at what she had done to Teodoro but relieved that the ordeal was finally over.

19

Epilogue

"I have to hear over the news that my little sister's life was in danger! What the hell, Kelly? I am putting you on the first flight out of that cursed place, and that is final!" bellowed Lenny, completely unhinged after he had watched the live news report.

"Lenny, I am fine. I didn't want to bother you with this because I had a whole team of people working to protect me. And I didn't want to endanger your life. I am very sorry for not telling you, but I only just got home. I was going to tell you all about it in a few days—"

"A few days? Are you kidding? I am going to hop on a plane right now and come to Spain and fetch your stubborn ass!" ranted Lenny. His face had turned a very disturbing shade of purple as he worked himself up into a full-scale big brother meltdown.

"So, is this a bad time to tell you that I am thinking of staying on in Spain a little longer?"

"KELLLLYYYY!" began the expected rant from Lenny.

"Relax, Len. I just need to show a lovely married couple a few cosy homes in Mojácar," explained Kelly rapidly.

"But..." Lenny tried to object.

"Oh, come on, Lenny. Trust me – nothing ever happens in Mojácar. What could possibly go wrong?"

ALMERIA MYSTERIES

Find out what happens next in...

Murder in Mojácar

Coming soon

For more information on the Almeria Mysteries series please visit:
www.almeriamysteries.com

Authors Note

Whilst this is a work of fiction, I have been inspired by the Almeria province in southern Spain and therefore many of the places visited by Kelly exist. I apologise to the wonderful residents for any minor changes to locations etc. for the purpose of the story.

One character, Kelly's distant relative Paula de Eguiluz, was a real person who lived during the late 1500s and early 1600s. The story of Paula and her trials for witchcraft is fascinating and shows how widespread was the persecution of women with certain skills. Healer or witch, Paula de Eguiluz certainly had the strength of character to be a great heroine.

Nika Grahame

2022

Printed in Great Britain
by Amazon

39099481R00096